A Horsey Honeymoon and Other Stories

Patricia Blanton Kavanagh

VANTAGE PRESS
New York

Cover design by Ximena Cajias

FIRST EDITION

Published by Vantage Press, Inc.
419 Park Ave. South, New York, NY 10016

Manufactured in the United States of America
ISBN: 0-533-14680-1

Library of Congress Catalog Card No.: 2003094594

0 9 8 7 6 5 4 3 2 1

To my late husband, Tom Kavanagh, and my eleven children

Contents

Prologue

Deep, Dark Woods

For him it was instant infatuation—"love at first sight" as they say. In the beginning, it was quite the opposite for me. In fact, I felt fear—apprehension, even repulsion.

It took many meetings before I was convinced that this was the real thing. I felt my love growing slowly. As happens occasionally, antipathy turned to acceptance and then a deep, almost violent passion—an obsession.

My turbulent emotions had overcome my reluctant intellect. My brain, however, persisted in cautioning me to weigh all the advantages and disadvantages before taking the final, fateful step.

Sometimes, when I thought what my future held for me if I risked the adventure, I broke out in a cold sweat, and trembled in an uncontrollable chill.

The climax was reached with the signing of the contract—there could be no turning back now. My heart beat wildly, dangerously as I realized I might have signed my death warrant.

For there were huge, untamed bears on the property. The land was so wild it would be quite easy to become hopelessly lost in its dense woods. Or there was the possibility of sinking dangerously deep in the hungry muck, which tried to swallow me up the first time I walked along the edge of the deceptively shallow-looking creek, which cut across the property. And then, Lake Michigan with its violent winter storms, its mammoth waves at any time, and only a few miles away, waiting to pounce on me and drag me back into its depths if I should happen to go swimming out too far. Or worse still, venture out in our small boat and be overturned in some unexpected, violent squall.

The land is surrounded by the raging lakes. Lake Michigan a few miles to the west. Lake Huron a few short miles to the east. And the Straits of Mackinac directly to the north. What if they should all overflow their boundaries in some great natural cataclysm? We would hopelessly, helplessly perish. For the land is near the very "Tip O' the Mitt." Practically under the Mackinac Bridge.

I agonized for two, nearly three years before agreeing to make my husband's fondest dreams come true. Would I be able to stand the isolation—the separation from family and old and very dear friends?

But this property, this particular plot of ground was so strikingly beautiful. Only a few miles from Harbor Springs, and its incomparable view of Little Traverse Bay and its own secure harbor, this land was so wildly, heartbreakingly beautiful, it could have been located in an undiscovered continent. It is composed of a profusion of hills and dales, high meadows and deep swamps. Some sections are thickly covered with hardwood forests of maples, oaks, aspens, birch and beech. An apple orchard crowns the top of the highest hill.

Other wild fruit trees and blackberry bushes flourish at random in open patches of meadows. Wild strawberry plants compete with tiny wild flowers for space in both shady and sunny spots on the dry and high ground. The brilliant yellow of the marsh marigold gleams like a bright promise of paradise in the deep dark mystery of the fragrant cedar swamp.

The brook wends its graceful way in unexpected twists and turns through meadows and swamps. At several spots it widens and deepens to form icy hiding spots for seductive trout, luring the fisherman to try his luck, casting his bait from the deep shade of magnificent green ferns.

At one spot the brook becomes a pond, a haven sheltered by magnificent towering hemlocks, spruce and pine. Deer, rabbits, and many species of birds have kept this plot of earth for a sanctuary since the days of the Indians. Dare we intrude on their privacy?

My thoughts hopscotched, bounding first in one direction, then another. They became unbalanced, veering too much one way, and then the other. And, ending like a game of hopscotch, exactly where they had begun. I had come to appreciate the land, but I was still in awe of it, still somewhat frightened of a life so far removed from the life of close interactions with friends. Could I accept a way of life so isolated?

There was no hesitation in my husband's mind. He had been crazy about the property from the first moment we drove by it on our way to visit our son in the Upper Peninsula. When Tom noticed the "For Sale" sign, he slammed on his brakes.

"I can't believe it!" he yelled. (He was looking at the lowest corner of the property—a deep, dark, dank cedar swamp.)

"Who would be crazy enough to sell this beautiful swamp?"

I was thinking to myself, "Who would be crazy enough to buy it?"

I had visions of snakes, even alligators lurking in the deep shadows of the cedars. The trees themselves appeared to me as sinister, forbidding warning posts. They seemed to say "Keep out—if you know what's good for you, and I do mean you!"

A Horsey Honeymoon

One of the jobs that helped put our daughter Bridget through Michigan State University was working in the horse barns during the winter months. She cheerfully shoveled horse manure during frigid eerie early hours, It was ambrosia to *her* nostrils because she was near those beloved horses!

Instead of being born with the proverbial silver spoon in mouth, Bridget must have been born with horseshoe in hand. Because she's crazy about horses. Always has been and always will be. This passion almost got her into trouble later on. When she was thirteen, the monies she earned baby-sitting went for riding lessons. All through high school, her summer job money was channeled in the same horsey direction.

When the boys began to notice her and ask her out on dates, she insisted they *not go* to movies, restaurants, concerts or bars, but horseback riding instead!

Her best poems and essays were about horses. She has a natural ability for writing and riding. By the time she was eighteen, she was a counselor and riding instructor at a summer camp in Michigan.

The next three summers she wrangled horses at a Montana dude ranch and led the Easterners on perilous paths through the mountains.

Naturally, when Bridget met and married her one and only Joedy, shortly after the ceremony and garden reception, they set off on their honeymoon to ride horseback on a Rocky Mountain ranch.

On the day the trip began, her dad and I were quite surprised when they drove up to our house in their pickup truck sporting the following garb:

They both wore Western-style clothing. Plaid shirts, blue jeans, cowboy boots, and cowboy hats. Instead of carrying a stylish purse as many brides do, Bridge lugged a beautiful saddle. Joedy had given it to her for one of her engagement presents.

They were traveling out West on special airline tickets, courtesy of a family member who worked for the airlines. I distinctly remembered the letter accompanying the tickets had stipulated dress clothes for both bearers of the tickets. I reminded her of this.

"Well," Bridge insisted, "we *are* dressed up. Western-style. I don't think we really have to wear fancy dudey Eastern garb. Anyway, who could refuse to let newlyweds board a plane for their honeymoon no matter how they're dressed?"

We piled all their gear into our old station wagon and took off for Detroit's Metro Airport. We dropped Bridge and Joedy at the most convenient entrance, blew one last kiss their way, and retraced our tire tracks to our office in Livonia.

The phone was ringing as my husband turned the key in the door. I grabbed the receiver before the answering device activated. Bridge's pleas, sobs, and moans nearly deafened my ear.

"Mom, you won't believe it! The agent won't honor our tickets because of the way we're dressed. He doesn't like our clothes. Says we're not dressed to code like it says in the letter. He says we're supposed to look like a lady and a gentleman."

"Bridge," I interrupted, "just get some fancier clothes out of your bags."

"But, Mother, you don't understand! We didn't *pack* any fancy clothes. We thought it wasn't important. You know I bought only jeans and plaid shirts for my trousseau. I didn't bring *any* of the pretty dresses you bought me. The last plane leaves in an hour. Do you think you and Dad could find some clothes for Joedy and me and get them out here in time?"

Find some clothes for them to wear? Bridge had been independent and living away from home for several years. None of her clothes were still available at our house. Her dad and I were both about forty years older and forty pounds fatter than the honeymooners, but I said, "Okay, Bridge, I'll do what I can. There are two bags for the charity pickup out on the front porch. Old clothes from some of your older siblings and their spouses. They're out of style, but they might fit you and Joedy. We'll try to retrieve them before the pickup and hope some of them will be okay."

Bridge went on, "I'll need a good dress and high heels, and Joedy needs a suit, dress shirt, shoes, socks, a belt, and tie. Please, Mom!"

We dashed home. I had my usual good luck. The two huge black plastic bags of old clothes and good will were still on the porch. Tom tore open one and I the other. He found a cast-off 1970s vintage 100 percent polyester suit from a son-in-law. Even though this suit had been scrunched into the corner of the bag, it was the type that *nothing* could wrinkle! The trousers would be quite loose and rather short on Joedy, but they *were* wrinkle-free.

Tom raced inside to scrounge up socks, a belt, shoes and tie for Joedy from his closet. I triumphantly wrenched a prize from my black bag—a polyester shirt also wrinkle-free and also from the son-in-law. It was one of about twenty donated to our family years ago when he edited his closet.

Now I galloped into the house and thumbed through my sentimental closet. The one full of my favorite dresses now years and inches too small for me.

I extracted a jewel. A beautiful East Indian silk print dress, all gold and rust. It was size five and would look great with

Bridge's golden sun-bleached hair and bright sweet-chocolate brown eyes. Our feet are still the same size, so my best high-heel black sandals would do for Bridge.

Back to the airport we roared with eyes and ears alert for cops. The nervous young honeymooners were waiting for us outside the proper door.

"Thanks so much, Mom," this from Bridge as she and I raced for the ladies' room and Tom and Joedy for the men's. The last jet for their honeymoon retreat was taking off in ten minutes! Bridge plunged into a booth and then began to sob, "Did I tell you I also have to wear stockings and a slip?"

"No, you *didn't* tell me, but take these," I said as I stepped into an adjoining booth and tore off my pantyhose and half-slip. I flung them over the top of my stall into hers. Luckily for her, the elastic on both was in good shape and shrunk to fit her.

Bridge's sobs stopped and giggles erupted.

"Oh well, this is sure a honeymoon we'll never forget." The Western garb was hastily stuffed into duffel bags. Then husband Tom and I nearly burst our hearts and lungs as our old legs tried to keep up with the kids. We four made it to the gate. Bridge in my four-inch heels and Joedy quite bizarre with the out-of-style suit with flapping loose trousers and a nice show of ankle.

The jet was ready to roll. We kissed and hugged the honeymooners. We gave a great sigh of relief as they finally ran down the jetway lugging duffels and saddle.

Tom and I were too mentally and physically exhausted to go back to the office. We turned the corner of our street in time to see the charity people collecting what was left of the two bags of clothes. "What a day!" said Tom. "I hope we don't have any more honeymoons for a while!"

The Kavanagh family celebrating the wedding of Bridget and Joedy in 1984.

Christmas Gifts for Michael

It was only eight o'clock in the morning, and already I had the dough for the Christmas cookies mixed and ready for the oven. I had planned to stay in the house all day and begin my Christmas preparations in earnest, but my daughter Bridget had changed all that.

She was afraid she would be late for school. She had missed the bus as she often did and her brother had warned her, "I'm not walking you to school one more time. It would make me late for my classes again."

Bridget's tears were real and were the only excuse I needed to escape from the house. I hastily threw on an old wraparound camel's hair coat over my nightgown, plunged my feet into an old pair of boots, and placed a tin of cookie dough in the oven. Bridget looked at me with big eyes.

"Oh, Mother! You're not going like that, are you?"

"Of course, why not?"

"What if somebody sees you?"

"I couldn't care less."

"Let's cut through the park, Mother. It'll save about five minutes."

At the end of our block is a park called "Lola Valley." Anyone who has never seen it cannot believe such a place exists in greater Detroit. It is a mood, a fairyland, another world. The entire park is an ancient riverbed, a soft, green, grassy-carpeted canyon.

On this gloriously gloomy December day, the chronic fog and mist with which the river bed is often permeated had embraced the lower level, transforming the always unreal and other-worldly atmosphere into a veiled meadow and forest, which seemed to float, a setting for a myth, a romance.

It seemed to me that my tiny little golden-haired daughter and I had intruded into and become part of a Watteau landscape. In these modern times, a small brook is all that remains of the ancient river.

The stream is outlined by enormous weeping willows. These willows as well as the elms and ancient maples, which make up the glens, were here centuries ago. They watched over young Indian children then just as our young ones seem to be guarded by the old trees today.

This was once an Indian campground. One of my sons had found an arrowhead close by the creek a few days ago. Now Bridget and I were climbing the stone steps after crossing the wooden bridge over the creek. The setting made my thoughts wander to another Indian campground. They call that place Bay City now.

But many decades ago, a young Irish boy played with Ojibway children in just such a camping ground as this. That place was surrounded by willows, which hugged the Saginaw River. Michael Daily was an orphan of eleven brought out West in 1837 from New York City by his only living relative in America.

She revealed herself to be an insensitive and unmaternal aunt. They came by boat along the Erie Canal. At some point there must have been a transfer to a lake ship because he often told his son in later years how his aunt left the ship at the Village of Saginaw. This was after she told him, "You're going to be on your own now, Michael. I can't be bothered with the care of an eleven-year-old boy."

The captain of the ship saw him standing alone, crying. When told he had not money to go farther, the captain signaled the lighthouse keeper at the lighthouse, which guarded the entrance to Saginaw Bay.

"Maybe the lighthouse keeper will let you stay with him. I've no room for an extra child on board," he said.

Young Michael was handed over to the keeper. He said to Michael, when the transfer was safely made in spite of heavy seas, "I'm sorry, laddie. You'd be better off back in Saginaw staying at the former blockhouse. I'll take you there."

The next day the keeper did escort Michael to "The Blockhouse," where the owner was very glad to have a young boy to help with chores. Because now the former Saginaw fort had become a tavern. The Indians were friendly now, and the French voyageurs and fur traders made their necessary stops for food and lodging at this place. Michael had a congenial and fascinating home at last. He received instruction in mathematics, English, and French, with the money he earned in his chore work at the tavern. He also carried the mail from Saginaw to Lower Saginaw (now Bay City) for a penny a letter. In winter he jogged on frozen Saginaw River to make the round trip.

There were no English-speaking children for Michael to play with, only a few French hunters and trappers and the Indians and their children. Michael was enchanted by these people. Born and reared in New York City, he was thrilled by the vast landscape of forest and the challenges of skimming the waters of Saginaw Bay and Lake Huron in a fragile canoe.

Michael was treated as a son by the Indian Chief. The Ojibways taught him how to survive in the forests. He learned to trap the fur-bearing animals and trade their furs. In a few years, he became a living legend of that land, a wealthy fur trader and landowner.

His Indian friends told him of a great store of furs coming down from northern Canada. These furs would be sold to the first reputable dealer to reach the trading post at Mackinac Island. Michael jogged all the way and beat a competitor to the prize, although the other man was traveling by a sleigh pulled by a fast and experienced team of dogs. This coup made Michael an extremely wealthy man. He married the daughter of a Frenchman. He was a prosperous landowner. After the required nine months, Michael and Agnes were expecting their first baby.

Only two weeks previously on a trip to Bay City, my uncle told me this story: "I remember a strange tale that was sometimes whispered about by older members of our family. About that time that your great-grandfather and his French wife were expecting a baby, an Indian maiden, the daughter of the chief, came to call at the now rich man's great house. She insisted on seeing him, but he would not speak to her."

Now as Bridget and I were nearing the end of our journey, other bits of information about this myth-maker formed a great situation in my mind. I imagined this girl, Michael's friend since childhood, knocking on the front door of the great Victorian mansion. It would have been a raw, damp day in mid-December. A day like this one. The girl's name was "Dancing Reed" because she had always been graceful even as a toddler learning to walk.

She knocked timidly at the door and asked to see Michael. When a French serving girl offered to show her into the house, she replied, "I will not enter the French woman's house, but I have something to say to Michael."

He refused to see her, saying, "I have nothing to say to her."

Dancing Reed received the reply stoically. She sat down on the front porch, huddled inside her brilliant red blanket. Her face was drawn and thin, but her body looked large and ungainly under the folds of the blanket. She sat there for twenty-four hours, refusing a bowl of ragout, which the French woman, taking pity on her, had offered her by the serving girl's help.

Finally, at the beginning of the second day, when snow began to fall, the day had become bleak and bitterly cold, she rose, pulled her blanket tightly about her, and walked slowly away, proud even in her awkward uncomfortable gait, her scarlet blanket a slash of color against the sullen gray sky.

The firstborn child, a son, was born to Michael and his wife, Agnes, a week before Christmas. A few days later, on Christmas Eve, the Indian Chief came to Michael's house for their annual exchange of Christmas gifts. He carried in his arms several bundles, gifts for his old friend Michael.

The Indian asked to see the new baby. Following the servant girl, he put his bundles down on the chaise lounge in Agnes's bedroom. Agnes was lovely to look at, with ivory-tinted skin. Her cheeks were pinker than usual, although she always had high color. She did not trust this Indian. Her eyes betrayed her alarm. Her full rosy lips began to tremble.

Agnes was propped up in her enormous beautifully carved bed. She held the tiny boy in her arms, his strong fist entangled in her long black hair.

"Let me hold the boy," said the Chief. "This babe is a handsome one. Let us trade," he suggested as he wrested the wee one from Agnes's grasp. He began rocking the baby in his arms, ignoring the shrill cries from Agnes.

"Give me back my son! Michael, make him hand Harry back to me!"

"I give you my new grandson; you give your son to me!"

The Indian pointed in the direction of the bundles on the lounge where two tiny fists emerged from a small red blanket and a loud wail added to the general hubbub. Agnes continued to sob. She trembled under the heavy counterpane. Her arms hungered to shield her son again.

Michael looked at her with one reassuring glance. "Do not fear, Agnes."

Then, with a respectful smile, he turned toward his friend, the Indian, "I am honored, O Chief of the Ojibways," he began. "I am honored that you would suggest this, but I am not worthy to bring up the grandson of the great Chief. He would sicken and die, away from the fresh air of the forest. He could never tolerate being confined in this stuffy house."

Agnes sighed and shut her eyes; tiny baby Harry relaxed and cuddled against the Chief, who was holding him in a vise-like grip.

* * *

Bridget and I had stepped out of the Watteau painting and left the French landscape far behind. We were nearing the school. Bridget looked at me and smiled. "Mother, you must be daydreaming. I've been talking to you and you haven't even answered me."

Her hair is blond, but her eyes are black and slightly slanted. Her cheekbones are as prominent as my own.

"I said you can go home now, Mother," she repeated.

"Your nightgown is peeking out under that old coat, and I don't want my friends to see you. They'd think I had a silly mother!"

I laughed and kissed her good-bye. I scurried home, taking the shortcut through the park. The fog was so thick now that it was almost impossible to pick my way over the bridge. Snow had begun to fall in great clumps. I kept slipping on the wet grass, which soaked my boots as I struggled up the steep hill out of the park.

It was a good morning to go back to bed and sleep awhile, I thought. I'd finish baking the cookies this afternoon. I stopped at the fireplace on the way to my bed. I added another log to the dying fire. In a few moments, the fire began to crackle again. I removed the perfect cookies from the oven and placed the extra dough in the fridge.

In my bedroom once again, I glanced in the mirror at my reflection. At my black hair and eyes. I sighed as I climbed into my bed. Was I part Indian? Had they traded babies or not?

Campaigning on Horseback

The young rider, my father, was weary and saddle sore. America had entered World War I on the side of the Allies, but the discovery of my father's extremely poor eyesight had prompted his honorable release from the U.S. Cavalry. Trying to get back into uniform, his war was now with the bureaucracy in Washington. He wanted to finish what he had begun with such high hopes.

In the meantime he hoped to win the position of Prosecuting Attorney of Scott County, Missouri. He needed the security and self-esteem the office would give him before he dared ask Maureen Daily of Bay City, Michigan, to marry him.

My father, whose name was Harry Blanton, campaigned on horseback. He covered the entire length of Scott County, visiting each farm home. He stopped at each house, shop, and tavern in every village and town and knocked on each door.

He told all who would listen how he had supported himself through his years at Old Western High in Georgetown and then Georgetown University Law School in Washington D.C. He explained how he had served in the U.S. Army and Cavalry. He promised each potential voter he would serve his constituents to the best of his ability and honor the laws of this country.

Often a farmer and his wife would invite my father to have dinner with them and spend the night in the "spare room" before continuing his journey. It was a long, hard trek through sunshine and stormy weather.

The country folk were impressed by my father's sincerity, intelligence, and energy. Most of the inhabitants of Scott County were of old Southern stock, their ancestors having come originally from Virginia or Kentucky. But there were also pockets of hardy German farmers. In spite of the fact that our country was in a bitter struggle with their forefathers' homeland, these farmers were devoted to America, rejoicing in the freedom they were guaranteed under our constitution. And they were held in high regard by their fellow farmers of Anglo-Saxon extraction.

Harry Blanton won the election and gave credit for his success to a great extent of the support and wit of Otto Shoen, the leading German politico in Scott County. Among Otto's efforts on my father's behalf was in the following incident.

In the last week before the November election, my father was asked to join a group of German farmers in Otto's tavern. There was a full house and my father's opponent, a wealthy established lawyer, was also present.

This fellow offered to treat all those in the place to as many drinks as they wanted. My father couldn't afford such a show of geniality and looked askance as the beer started to flow. But Otto smiled at my father and said in German to the assembled crowd, "Take this man's drinks, but vote for Harry Blanton!"

While fulfilling his term as Prosecuting Attorney, my father continued his attempts to reenter the army. He was rewarded for his efforts. The war had taken a heavy toll, and now his poor eyesight did not prevent his acceptance to Officer's Training School. The U.S. Army needed all the men it could get. He married his Maureen in February 1918, and after the Armistice was signed in November of 1918, he returned to the practice of law.

My father became a famous trial lawyer. President Roosevelt appointed him Federal District Attorney for the Eastern

District of Missouri, with headquarters in St. Louis. While serving that capacity for twelve years, my father won every case except one. He originated the Missouri Plan for Selection of Judges. He was responsible for the establishment of beautiful Riverfront Park in St. Louis with its graceful Jefferson Memorial Arch, also called *The Gateway to the West.* The Old Cathedral and Old Court House of St. Louis were saved thanks to his farsightedness.

Michigan Memories

"Help! Oh, help!" Frank screamed. The breakers rolled over the nine-year-old, muffling his cries. He knew he was drowning. He fought for his life, clawing his way to the surface twice only to disappear beneath the water each time.

Only one young man in the crowd of merrymakers at the beach party saw his struggle. Fred Wendland rushed to Frank Daily's aid. He dragged the boy from the water, then performed artificial respiration, saving his life.

My Uncle Frank had tried to impress my mother Maureen's friends with his swimming prowess and gone out too far in Saginaw Bay. This drama took place in 1912 and was one of Grandma Daily's favorite Linwood Beach stories. She and Grandpa had supervised the building of the Shamrock, a large cottage at Linwood Beach on Saginaw Bay around the turn of the century.

The cottage was painted green and white and built in three sections like a shamrock. Great-grandma Lewis's antique pine furniture filled the rooms. Kerosene lamps and the fires in the fireplaces furnished soft glowing light at night.

On the first floor, a cozy entrance hall greeted visitors. This opened to a large living room with a stone fireplace on the left and an equally large dining room also with a stone fireplace on the right. A well-furnished kitchen spread across the back of the Shamrock. A spacious porch circled the house.

The upstairs consisted of a long hallway and six large bedrooms. A balcony across the front of the Shamrock overlooked Saginaw Bay. Another large balcony stretched across the length of the house and was the gathering place for the servants and children during rest periods. From there we could see the commuter Detroit and Mackinaw trains picking up or unloading fathers and grandfathers on their return from the city at the end of the day. Some of the men, like my Grandpa Daily, preferred to drive their own cars out to Linwood from Bay City each night.

My sisters Rosemary, Maureen, and Anne and brothers John and Joe and I were privileged to accompany our mother Maureen to this wonderful cottage every summer of our early childhood.

Those were busy, happy days. We learned to swim, paddle a canoe, row a boat, and ride horseback. Grandma laid down strict rules for our safety. Chief among these was: "Stay away from the railroad tracks behind the cottage. You are forbidden to even go near them!"

I must have been a really obnoxious sissy because every red-blooded American kid at Linwood Beach except me was attracted to the Detroit and Mackinaw railroad tracks like chewing gum is attracted to high-heeled shoes.

One day when we were very young, my older sister Rosemary and a friend asked me to join them in a railroad scheme. Remembering Grandma's stern admonitions, I said a loud "No!" I preferred the taunts of "Sissy, sissy!" from Rosemary to upsetting my grandma. And anyway, I didn't want to end up mangled on the D & M railroad tracks.

So I stood on the sidelines as my older sister and her friend went about their adventure.

A short time before the D & M freight train was due to speed past our cottage, Rosemary and Betty took several straight sewing pins, crossed them, then ran up to the tracks, and placed them on the rails. Then they ran as fast as their little legs could carry them and hid behind the green ice house while the train roared by. When they thought it was safe, they ran back to the tracks and picked up their pins.

Their squeals of delight showed their experiment was successful. Rosemary screamed, "Oh look! All of mine turned out perfect! Four darling pairs of scissors for my dolls!"

The green ice house that had sheltered Rosemary and Betty was duplicated behind most of the cottages. The ice house was filled with blocks of ice protected and preserved by sawdust. Grandpa, Uncle Frank, and the other cottagers had cut the ice from frozen Saginaw Bay during the previous winter and stored it for the summer when it was used to keep the "ice boxes" cold and preserve the food that Grandpa brought out from the city.

Grandpa was a partner in the wholesale grocery business of Tanner & Daily in Bay City. Every night he drove his very large automobile, laden with groceries, out to the cottage.

We children waited for the sound of his horn, "aaaaaaah-ooooooogha, aaaaaaah-ooooooooooogha!" and then came tearing from all directions to help him unload the car and carry in the groceries. Grandpa's car was a Cadillac, and Grandma drove an old-fashioned electric car. Electric cars had been very fashionable and very expensive about 1904 when she learned to drive. But they were no longer stylish in the twenties when we children enjoyed our summers at the Shamrock.

Grandma didn't care what the styles were—she made her own style!

Her electric car looked like an old-fashioned carriage from the 1800s minus the horses, but she continued to drive it until 1945 when she broke her hip at the age of eighty-four.

Grandpa had a stall made for her electric in the ice house. He had an electric battery charger installed to recharge the battery for her on the grand occasions when she fearlessly drove her car all the way to the Shamrock from Bay City. I can see her now—cutting in and out of traffic, astonishing the drivers of big automobiles and trucks, which towered above her. Once a bemused truck driver actually teased her with the old cliché and yelled, "Get a horse!"

One summer when I was about eight, I spent many hours building a whole medieval village out of wet sand. There was a protective castle with walled enclosures, village houses, moat and river. I landscaped the set-up with pretty little trees that my mother advised me were really poison ivy plants.

On sunny days we children spent most of the time on the beach or in the water, jumping the breakers. Or swimming out to the raft where we dove back into the water and raced each other back to shore again.

Our mother was an excellent swimmer and Grandma and Grandpa were still good swimmers in the twenties. I can picture him now in this two-piece bathing suit heading down through the yellow sand toward the dock and water. One summer he had hurt one leg in an accident and received compensation from his insurance company. He limped in the city, but I soon noticed that he forgot to limp at the beach. I called out to him, "Grandpa, you forgot to limp on your insurance leg!" Grandma still had a gorgeous figure in her sixties. She preferred swimming at dusk because it was hard to see then. She said, "I don't want men staring at me!"

At night we built campfires on the beach and roasted hot dogs and marshmallows. Maybe that's why I still prefer roasted hot dogs burnt and with a little sand on them for flavor.

Around the mysterious firelight, Grandpa conjured visions of his pioneer father, Michael Daily. He regaled us with tales about the earlier days near Saginaw and Lower Saginaw (as Bay City was called then). He told us how he accompanied his father through the deep forests to visit the Ojibway Indian Chief. A silent Indian figure had paced them through the shadows and then stopped, stared at them and smiled. He called out something in the Ojibway tongue. Michael reassured

Grandpa, "The Indian said, 'Father and son! Don't be afraid.' "

Grandpa added more logs to the fire and as the sparks shot into the black sky told us more of Michael's boyhood days.

"In 1836 when my father was only twelve and an orphan boy from New York City, his aunt brought him out to Michigan on the Erie Canal. He lived at a tavern called, 'The Blockhouse.' It had been the fort at Saginaw. My father carried the mail from Saginaw to what is now Bay City along frozen Saginaw River. He was not much older than you children. He received a penny a letter, and it took him a day to make the trip each way. When he was older, he jogged all the way to Fort Mackinaw at the straits and beat another man who was racing him by fast dog sled."

Grandpa sang old French songs in a singsong, off-key voice. He sang in the old French Canadian patois he had learned from his French mother, Agnes Loncquetin.

Grandma told stories about her Scottish uncles' adventures as lumberjacks in the forests and camps of Michigan. She told of her early days as a teacher at the Raby school near the Saginaw River.

"When I began to teach school," she said, "some of my male students were taller and older than I was. I had to outwit them and keep them interested in learning. But I let them have something to look forward to as often as I could so they wouldn't give up and drop out of school. I declared a recess every time my friend Captain Jenkins's ship, *the Arundal*, came into view from the windows. Captain Jenkins sounded the ship's whistle, 'toot, toooot, toooooot!' and all the kids yelled, 'Hooray! *The Arundal*, *The Arundal*,' and blasted out of that little schoolhouse!"

One night when we were telling tales around a campfire, one of the adults, a guest we really didn't know well, told a ghost story. It was very scary and ended with the dead man screaming, "Give me back my gold arm, give me back my gold arm."

This story frightened me so completely that I couldn't sleep that night. I was afraid the ghost would appear in my room at any minute and demand his arm! I cried and cried. The sound of the waves crashing against the shore outside my windows had always comforted me, but this night it terrorized me. It sounded threatening and evil.

My grandma's room was next to mine and she heard my sobbing. She took me into her bed where I felt safe from the ghost looking for his golden arm as well as crashing waves.

I'll always remember the luncheon that Grandma gave for my sisters, my cousins, and me. She decorated the long table at the Shamrock with graceful grapevines, wild flowers, and beautiful fruit scattered about the highly polished table.

She used her antique blue-and-white willow china and blue glasses. She gave each of us a dollar at the end of the delicious lunch of sandwiches, fruit, cocoa, nuts and sour cream cookies.

When I was ten years old, a group of eight cottages at Linwood Beach burned down in a fierce winter storm. The sons of the cottage families came to Linwood Beach to ice-fish and ice-boat on frozen Saginaw Bay. They built a great fire in their cottage fireplace. Sparks from the fire were flung by high winds to their roof and ignited an inferno. The fire raced up bare overhanging tree branches and spread from cottage to cottage before help could arrive from neighboring Linwood Village.

The Shamrock burned to the ground, the house and everything in it gone forever. But I'll always have my memories. "My Michigan Memories."

Easter Memories

Alleluia, alleluia, let the joyful anthem rise
And the choirs of heaven chant them in the temples of the skies
Let the mountains skip with gladness and the joyful valleys ring
With hosannas in the highest to Our Savior and Our King.
Alleluia, alleluia, He is risen as He said, etc.

I may not have remembered all the phrases of this Easter hymn correctly after sixty years, but I do remember thinking when I was only six, that those mountains couldn't have been more excited than my sisters and I were on Easter morning.

We grew up in a strict religious family, and the sacred aspect of Easter was always emphasized. We usually went to early Mass and often sang that beautiful Easter hymn on our way home from church as a glorious sunrise spread its rosy rays at the northern end of the Missouri Bootheel.

Mother and Daddy celebrated the holiday spirit of Easter too, and they always made the day a very special time of fun and beauty for us children. Springs came early to southeast Missouri, and if the radio predicted sunshine for Easter morning, my dear mother could rise at five o'clock, hurry outside in the dewy darkness, and place several dozen brightly colored hen's eggs among the purple and pink hyacinths, yellow jonquils, and red tulips, which bloomed near the driveway under the watchful protection of a huge old magnolia tree.

Mother knew that we little girls would be awake early and run outside in bathrobes and bedroom slippers with our empty Easter baskets swinging from our arms to the accompaniment of robins' songs and the sad calls of the mourning doves.

Often wild rabbits scurried across the lawn as we raced toward the flower beds, looking for our eggs. We were sure one of these rabbits was the REAL Easter Bunny!

If the day was predicted to be rainy or too chilly, Mother held our private Easter-egg hunt indoors. She hid the eggs in a few easy places, but mostly in hard-to-find places, so the adventure would be a challenge. One year she hid some of the eggs too well. Several of them weren't found for weeks.

Finally the spoiled-egg aroma wafted out from the bottom drawer of Mother's prized secretary desk in the living room. There we found three turquoise eggs hiding under some old family letters.

I was a very shy preschooler and didn't make friends easily like my more outgoing sisters did. One Easter weekend, my older sister and my younger sister kept running to the front door repeatedly. The brass doorknocker kept banging as their little friends appeared on the flagstone porch bearing the pretty little "twenty-five cent baskets" to give to my sisters. I had seen the baskets at the dime store and knew how much they cost. Each sister had three baskets from friends, and I had none.

When the last knocking had produced another basket for my sister, I burst into tears and ran upstairs to cry in my bedroom. My dear Grandma Daily, who was visiting us, heard my crying and sized up the situation at once.

She called a taxicab, went into town, and returned in a few minutes with a "fifty-cent basket" from the dime store for me! In the twenties when all this took place, fifty cents was a lot of money. Grandma beckoned to me to follow her to her bedroom where she presented me with my gift. My new basket was truly elegant and much larger than the twenty-five cent ones my sisters had received. Grandma told me to tell my sisters that my basket was from my secret pal if they wanted to know who had given it to me. I thanked Grandma for my wonderful gift and ran downstairs. I placed my very large basket next to their smaller ones. Grandma had followed me downstairs to see the action. She sat down in her favorite wing chair next to the fireplace and picked up a book, which she pretended to read.

Soon one of my sisters came running into the living room. I could no longer contain my happiness and yelled, "See what I got!"

I pointed to my wonderful basket. My sister stared at the beautiful big basket full of Easter goodies in disbelief.

"Where did you get that 'fifty-cent basket'?" she asked.

"From my secret pal," I answered with a smile.

I knew that behind her book Grandma was smiling as well.

Outwitted

My grandma, with a high-school diploma and two years of college work behind her, considered herself very well-educated for the 1890s. My grandpa, although a very wealthy successful businessman, had only an eighth-grade education.

Grandma once asked him for forty dollars to buy a pretty lamp that she fancied. Grandpa took his checkbook from his pocket with a flourish, began to write a check, and then hesitated. "Mary," he said, "I'm not sure I know how to spell forty."

"Well, Harry," she replied, "do you know how to spell fifty?"

Valentine's Day

My mother always made much of St. Valentine's Day. She fashioned a beautiful valentine container from an old hat box. She decorated it with white paper and red hearts. Then she cut a big slit in the lid for little fingers to put their valentines in. Every year we children were busy for days making valentines for our family from red construction paper, ribbons and paper doilies for lace. We wrote immortal original rhymes on each one.

On February fourteenth, Mother's sweet voice would awaken us as she went to each bedroom: "Happy Valentine's Day! Children, here are your cards!"

Later on I realized Valentine's Day was not all sweetness and light as Mother had made it at home. The following are excerpts from my diary when I was twelve in 1934: "Feb. 14. I didn't get any valentines from boys except from Emmanuel, Norman, Grainy, and Frederick. But then, what could I expect? Those are the only boys in my class."

At that time our family lived in Sikeston, a small country town in southern Missouri. I attended parochial school and there were, indeed, very few boys or girls in my class. The next year was more exciting. Our family moved to St. Louis, the largest city in Missouri. There were plenty of boys to send me valentines. I was thirteen and ready for romance as shown by my diary notation for that year, 1935:

"Feb. 14. I got a lot of valentines from boys this year. In fact, every boy in my class sent me one except Robert Senkosky. And he's the one I really like. But I did get valentines from eighteen boys. And two from Vincent Fagin. So maybe I should like him instead. I know he likes me. One day he threw twenty-five spitballs at me before Sister noticed and made him stand in the corner. And at recess he said: 'Sikesville, you kill me!' Whatever that means. I guess it means he really loves me because then he knocked me down to the ground. But then he helped me up. I only got a little bit hurt, so I didn't tattle on him. And it proves he really does love me and maybe I do love him instead of Robert Senkosky!"

All Aboard! All Aboard for St. Louis! All Aboard!

In these times when only a very small minority of Americans take advantage of our Amtrak system, and the vast majority have never ridden on a train, it is pleasant to recall the days when riding a train was very much a part of so many people's lives.

When I was a child in the "twenties," our family spent time every summer on the "sleepers" of the Wabash Cannonball or Michigan Central Railroad traveling between St. Louis, Missouri, and Detroit, Michigan.

I had occasion to board an Amtrak train to Chicago recently and couldn't help compare the present situation with the way things used to be. Instead of the dusty, empty, decrepit shell it is now, the station was filled with scores of active people, coming and going in the old days.

The trips on the trains were the high points of our busy summers. From the moment we heard the conductor call, "All aboard, all aboard!" we were in a constant state of excitement.

We got on the train in St. Louis. We went to Michigan to visit our grandparents. And then at the end of the summer, we would make the return trip to St. Louis from Detroit.

Soon after boarding the train, the whole bunch of us, mother and little children of stair step sizes, would head for the dining car. "Dinner in the Diner" was the best part of the whole trip. We ran through the cars when Mother would give us the "go ahead" signal—shutting our eyes as we made the long jumps across the scary, jiggling platforms, which connected one car to the next.

The smiling waiter serving my favorite whitefish (balancing his tray so gracefully as the train swayed back and forth), the finger bowls afterward, the hustle-bustle of the stylishly dressed ladies and gentlemen with their animated conversation and laughter—these were all part of the excitement.

Also, I must admit we children enjoyed being the center of attention, as most heads would turn to watch our group marching in. We usually had matching outfits and displayed our best manners. In those days children were considered an asset and were cherished and admired.

After dinner, we loved watching the porter make up our berths; it was just as thrilling every year and every trip, although we had seen it many times before. It was so hard dressing and undressing in the berths, especially if we had drawn an "upper berth." But bumping our heads and being thrown around by the motion of the train were just part of the fun. And we loved stuffing the clothes we had taken off in the green fish-net clothes hammocks.

My sister Maureen and I had saved our allowances of weekly quarters for a month or so in preparation for this trip. We invested our money in candy, which we hoarded to eat in our berths during the nightlong trip between St. Louis and Detroit. When Maureen and I were lucky enough to get a lower berth, we spent most of the night peeking out the windows and waving to the people getting on and off the train as well as the people working at the stations where we stopped during the night.

We munched our candy off and on all night long, unknown to our mother. We had no trouble getting back to sleep in between stops because the rhythmic rolling and swaying of the cars rocked us back to sleep in a few minutes. The CLANG-CLANG-CLANG as we approached crossings and the regular CLIKKEDY-CLACK CLIKKEDY-CLACK as we raced along the tracks through the night made a happy melody and background for our childish dreams.

"The train's backing into the stations! The train's backing into the station!" we children would yell the next morning as our train neared the terminal.

"Is everyone ready to get off? Have you all washed your faces and combed your hair?" Mother would ask.

We usually ate breakfast at the station because we seldom had time to get it over with on the train. Our Uncle Lewis Daily always met our incoming train at Detroit and then helped Mother transfer her brood of three, four, or more to the "Pere Marquette" train headed for Bay City, Michigan, after treating us to a filling breakfast in the terminal dining room.

On one memorable summer morning, Uncle Lewie ordered large bowls of hot oatmeal for all of us children. It was a standing rule in our family that food was not to be wasted—even oatmeal. We were expected to eat everything put in front of us at mealtime and all of it!

Now, Maureen and I had been eating candy all through the night before, so it's no wonder Maureen announced after gazing at the big bowl of oatmeal and getting a whiff of its rich sticky-sweet aroma.

"I don't feel so good. I don't think I can eat that oatmeal!" Maureen was Uncle Lewie's favorite, and he didn't want her to "get it" for not eating her breakfast.

"I'll give you a dollar if you eat your oatmeal, honey," he tried.

Never before in her life had Maureen been offered so much money at one time. She plunged her spoon into the offending oatmeal. She finished it off and then held her hand out to Uncle Lewie for the promised dollar. Then she proceeded to lose her breakfast—back into the cereal bowl.

Many years later when I was married and living in Detroit and blessed with an ever growing family, I would occasionally make the trip back to St. Louis by train—usually with the help of my mother.

One summer evening, she, my husband Tom, and I were loaded down with three little girls, dolls, teddy bears, luggage, and bags of bottles and diapers, rushing through the old Michigan Central Station, trying to get on our train before it pulled out on its merry way to St. Louis.

We shoved the two toddlers aboard, and I stepped up on the platform between cars, carrying the baby Deda, and bag of her bottles. It was then my mother announced, "I'd better check and see if I still have our tickets! See! My purse has come open! Oh Dear! Here's the envelope but the tickets are gone! They must have fallen out!"

The conductor began to call, "All aboard! All aboard for St. Louis! All aboard!"

My mother and my husband tore back through the great crowds of people rushing in the opposite direction, trying to get onto their trains on time. The floor of the terminal was littered with thousands of scraps of paper and old tickets, discarded and trampled on. Mother jogged determinedly along, her mouth set purposefully, a grim but positive look to her face, her eyes glued to the floor. Tom was a nervous wreck, having despaired, "You'll never find them in all that trash, Mother!" Tom yelled above the din of people shouting, trains puffing, and engine bells tooting.

"Hooray! There they are! I've found them!" she exulted as she swooped low and extracted them from a pile of refuse on the floor of the waiting room.

My husband practically carried my mother back to the train, which had begun to move slowly but surely out of the station. Meanwhile, I was pleading with the conductor to stop the train as my two toddlers cried out, "Where's Gramma? Where's Gramma? Is she lost? Oh, where's Gramma?"

Tom boosted Mother onto the observation car, wiped his perspiring forehead, blew kisses to us all, then headed for the nearest bar! Our trips were more than he could stand!

That trip was just a taste of what was to come. Several years and children later, my father invited me and all the children (nine by this time) to Missouri for a month's summer vacation—

"I'll pay your railroad fare," he wrote, "It's been a long time since the children have been down."

It was true—while four of the older children had made regular trips by plane to visit their grandparents, the five younger ones had never been to Missouri. I agreed to attempt the journey.

We had made reservations for two full-sized bedrooms. The days of single berths lining the aisles were long gone.

The hardest part of this trip was persuading little Rosemary and Annie even to get on the train. Somewhere they had heard tales of the devil and "Hell." They screamed and cried when they saw the huge, strange-looking engine of the train. Rosemary screamed, "It's a monster! It's a monster! I'm not going near that monster!"

Annie yelled, when the engine began puffing great clouds of steam, "What's that hot white stuff? Is this Hell? I don't want to go to Hell?" No reassuring from me could persuade them to get aboard. Finally, the conductor picked up a struggling little girl in each arm and placed them inside the train for me.

Luckily we had already eaten an early supper at home, so didn't have to attempt that trek to the diner with nine children. But the night was something else.

I had decided to keep Sean, the baby, and three of the more enterprising children with me in one room, while the other five children shared the three berths in the big bedroom next to us.

Little Rosemary was fascinated by the washbowl-toilet combination. It was necessary to shut the washbowl into the wall before the toilet appeared in the space underneath. Rosemary kept slamming the washbowl into the wall, splashing water all over the floor. She also thought it was fun to constantly flush the toilet.

Then she discovered the buttons. There they were, all in a nice neat row. Of course, she had to find out what would happen when she punched each one. One turned the lights off and on. The next turned on the air-conditioning. The fan came on next. Last and most exciting of all was the porter's bell. Rosemary kept punching them all in turn, all night long in between slamming the washbowl into the wall and flushing the toilet.

Annie had an unfortunate habit of constantly opening and shutting the door to the outside aisle of the train. Especially when one of the other little ones was actually on the toilet and curious travelers were passing by and peeking into our room.

As an accompaniment to this long night's journey into day, Rosemary's very, very favorite thing to do became punching the porter's bell. She thought it was very funny to see the little Japanese man appear immediately after she punched the button and say as he bowed, "You ling, Missy?"

The fourth time Rosemary summoned him, he was still smiling although in a puzzled sort of way.

"Folks next door," he began, "they keep me hopping, too! Five children in there with no father or mother at all!" He turned to me, "Missy, you know anything about this situation?"

I answered, "That situation is just part of this situation!"

That trip on the train was the last one I attempted with the whole family for obvious reasons. It was too much, even for me!

Winter

Marshmallow frosting covers the land
Covers the skyscrapers, the factories, our homes
Covers the side roads and the interstate band,
The interstate ribbons, the interstate bow.
Drab-feathered balls, which should have flown South
Cling for warmth on bright neon signs, on telephone wires,
On gray chimney tops, on black factory stacks.
Belching smoke through the snow.
Bitter winds stab at old ladies' skirts,
Making them wish they'd put on their slacks.
Neighbors help each other shovel each walk
They snow-blow their driveways, then gather and talk.

A World War II Honeymoon

Our wartime wedding ceremony in Fort Myers, Florida, was over. Tom and I saw my mother to her train and then took the cab to the Royal Palm Hotel where Tom had arranged accommodations for us.

This hotel was a beautiful old place (sort of like Petoskey's Stafford's Perry Hotel). It had seen better days but was glamorous enough for us.

Before she had left, I told Mother where we were staying on our honeymoon. She said, "Why, that's the hotel where your great-aunt Sarah was the bookkeeper many, many years ago." The old hotel had a beautiful big lobby with a bright fire in the fireplace at the end of the room the first chilly night we were there. At dinner, classical music was always played.

One night soon after our arrival, while in the dining room, I looked over at the table next to ours. I recognized the familiar face of movie star Jeanette MacDonald and her husband, Airman Gene Raymond, who was stationed at Buckingham Army Air Field with Tom. Not being especially shy, I dashed over to their table and got their autographs on my menu.

As far as the real part of the honeymoon went, I appeared the first night to Tom's amazement in a gorgeous, very seductive black lace night gown—one that I had received at one of my wedding showers. But this was a mistake. The gorgeous looking gown was very scratchy and itchy and not a plus for presenting me as a docile bride. I spent most of the night fighting the stylish black garment. Tom to the rescue . . . he returned to the hotel after his hours of flying the next day with extra large but comfortable looking G.I. pajamas for his bride. I wore them consistently from then on, and they were not very flattering but much more comfortable and not the least bit scratchy like the black job.

On the two Sundays we were in Fort Myers, we attended Mass where we enjoyed the sermons of Rev. Father J.J. O'Reardon, who had performed our wedding ceremony. He was a native of old Ireland. One of the admonitions he gave was: "Now, young men, ye who are soon to be actively engaging in war, although ye've always been told *not* to fight, and it's *wrong* to fight. Now—I'm telling ye, if ye *have* to fight, make sure ye can lick 'em!"

Soon Tom had his orders to travel to Greensboro, North Carolina, a processing center. From there he would be sent to his port of debarkation.

But first we had to change his trains in Jacksonville, Florida. Tom was afraid we would miss our connection because the first train was late. He said, "Come on, honey, take my hand and I'll pull you with me. We'll have to run through this train yard to the track where the train for North Carolina is ready to roll!" With that we raced through the train yard—going through several trains at their connecting spots between cars—he yanking me along in my high heels. We made it on time.

But when we reached the train for North Carolina, exhausted and breathless, there was another problem. Tom had ordered a big, comfortable lower berth for us. However, the conductor on the North Carolina-bound train said our wishes were impossible to fulfill. He had given us two narrow, uncomfortable upper berths one for Tom, one for me, on opposite sides of the aisle. Tom's years of high school basketball and then football at Notre Dame had developed his muscles so well that like a giant grasshopper he made the leap with the greatest of ease.

The next morning we said good-bye with passionate hugs and kisses through salty tears. As he left the train in North Carolina, I went to Washington, D.C. to spend a few days with my dear Aunt Catherine and then returned to St. Louis. There my parents would give me, as well as my sister with her children, a home again until, hopefully, our husbands returned to us at war's end.

The Apartment

The apartment was on Spring Street, in Soho.
It was six long flights up,
There was no elevator.
At the fourth floor, I stopped for breath
Leaning against the grimy, olive drab walls
Then—went on again for two more flights.

At each landing, we saw through open doors
The friendly faces of people seated about kitchen tables
Eating or playing cards;
All the apartment doors opened into kitchens.

David and Deda's was large, bright, and welcoming us.
The walls and ceilings painted a soft yellow.
Deda had sewn curtains of some flimsy, pale yellow material,
Which moved and danced about the open windows.

The conversation piece in the kitchen
Was the old-fashioned claw-footed bathtub
Painted white and hidden, when not in use,
By the kitchen sink and work center.

I tested it, soaking and enjoying every minute;
Couldn't decide whether I felt more like Cleopatra
At her perfumed bath, or some staunch pioneer woman
Taking a Saturday night special.

A knock at the kitchen door made me take mental notes;
Perhaps a curtain or screen when the budget allowed it.
The situation could prove
Embarrassing.

They had painted the rest of the apartment white
David dragged a sanding machine up the six flights of stairs
And sanded the living-room floor himself.
Both had polished and buffed till it glowed and glimmered
Like the ice-skating pond at the end of our block
Where Deda used to skate when she was a tiny little girl.

Deda had stripped and refinished the elegant second-hand
China cabinet, bought at a Salvation Army store.
David and a friend had lugged it up
The steep flights of stairs.

The cabinet held their treasures,
Books, whimsies, unusual mementos, from Germany, Ibezia,
From the days in Paris when both were students
At Marceau's Ecole Internationale de Mime.

There were two windows in this room
One, happy with a green-growing plants in hanging brass containers
Or in clay pots on the ledge
Needed no curtain.

The other window, opened to the cool air,

A fresh gossamer white curtain blew in and out
Waving to the people moving about
On the sidewalk and street far below.

The Other Apartment

From the window we could see the apartment building
Directly across the street. It was a one-time
Elegant affair with delicate wrought-iron balconies
Covering the symmetrically designed facade
Now a dirty white brick.

It reminded me
Of some decadent old dowager's costume—
Decorated with fine black lace collar and cuffs,
But sadly in need of a washing and mending.

The Cast Party

Terry, Deda, Tex, and I went to the party
One of the cast members gave it
In his ground-floor apartment
Only a block from Deda and David's.

The walls were white painted brick
Lined with shelves of books;
A fine antique oriental rug
Covered the hardwood floor.

Charles had flung a silken Spanish shawl
Over the grand piano. As more and more
People arrived and crowded around the piano
And table laden with soul food, oriental dishes and

Fine imported wines the shawl was brushed aside.
He had used it to cover mars and scratches as
My mother used to do with her piano when we
Were children and she had large crowds in for parties.

Someone put on some old Motown records from
the sixties and the wild and happy gyrations,
Which always accompany the real Motown Sound, began.
Five or six of us began to dance; the others pushed

Out to the edges making room for the dancers.
Wine glasses and bottles moved freely to and from
Hands and lips and tables. No one was smoking grass
Except two young boys. They offered me a drag.

I laughed—refused it. My son Terry looked at me
In surprise. "Watch out, Mom, I don't think
You can stand too much of this dancing!"
Deda just laughed. She had been to parties with me before.

Neither had any way of knowing I had been a
Prime stagline mover at many proms—Annapolis, Yale,
Georgetown, and Old Mizzou. Deda, still in her leotards
From her performance at the theatre, now danced solo.

While we all clapped in rhythm and admiration.
Several Puerto Rican Mime students began to dance
With us. A pretty Japanese girl's eyes smiled at me.
Was it Yoko Ono? Someone said she had been at the Mime
performance.

The party began to break up. It was four A.M.
Some people were kissing old friends good-bye.
Others were still kissing new friends hello. It

had been a great party. Too bad David wasn't there

But he was opening in Hartford. We walked back to
The apartment, Terry, Deda and I singing Christmas carols
As Tex turned somersaults and cartwheels down the center of deserted Spring Street!

Manhattan

I wonder why all the dreamers
Stay on in the city long after
The dream has become a nightmare
Then the nightmare, too, has vanished
Leaving only a vacuum
Leaving only the city
The vacuum
And the dreamers
Who have forsaken
Been forsaken by dreams.

Milk in a Whiskey Bottle

Once airborne, being aboard the 747 was a calming dream, and the action at John F. Kennedy slipped gradually into our deep memory. Sleep began to beguile the group, one by one. As the others slept, I began remembering all the plans Rosemary had laid to go back to Ireland. She had wanted to see, again, the wonderful young man who had won her heart on a trip to the *Old Sod* on spring break from Pratt Institute the previous March. She had been smitten with Scottie's charm and hoped to marry him some day. Now it was all coming true.

Rosemary, Scottie, and a bridesmaid from New York who had come a few days early, met us at Shannon. Rosemary looked beautiful as ever, her emerald-green eyes sparkling and her speech already carrying a bit of lilting brogue. We hugged and kissed midst tears and laughter. The huge box of china was presented and received with screeches of joy at Benner's Hotel, an ancient establishment patronized by the native Irish. It was a very cozy place, with a cheery fire always burning in the ancient fireplace in the lobby. Benner's was directly adjacent to St. John's Church, where the wedding was to take place, and was our home for the next few days.

Next morning was the wedding. Our host at the Inn, as well as the best man, Scottie's brother Jerry, warned us that it is protocol to keep the groom waiting for at least ten minutes. Observing this little ritual of pseudo-reluctance, the bride and bridesmaids trooped into the tiny barroom off the lobby and had a short drink to keep up Rosemary's courage "to do things *Irish.*"

The wedding Mass was lovely, under a stunning portico supported by marble pillars. Scottie had ordered big bouquets of lavender flowers to match the bridesmaids' dresses. Scottie's sister Margaret—an opera singer, no less—sang the solos. My lovely Rosemary and her handsome Scott spoke their vows and exchanged rings. She had married her Irish prince charming. And my Dudley Thomas was one very proud father in his spanking new suit.

The reception was at Benner's, with Margaret who had recently won the "Voice of Ireland" award, thrilling us with both ballads and popular songs. Scott's brother Aiden, a classical composer and national dance champion, gave the guests an exhibition of classical Irish folk dancing. Two of Scott's other brothers played instruments in a quartet. Rosemary had married a member of "*The Musical O'Carrolls, the premier musical family in Ireland.*" Scott sang a few songs, too, in his brilliant tenor voice.

Since we had come thousands of miles to Tralee to be present at Rosemary's wedding, and she was afraid she was facing many years of separation from her family, Rosemary insisted we share her honeymoon. You read right—we were to share her honeymoon. Only in Ireland. An idea seeming normal only to my delightful daughter. She and Scott had rented a cottage with a thatched roof and turf-burning fireplace in the main room. The cottage was near the ancient village and castle of Carragahault in County Clare. It was the first time any of us had been on someone else's honeymoon.

The main room was used for both eating and living. This small house slept eight, comfortably. Honeymooners on the second floor, others below. The cottage was equipped with central heating as a backup in case we wished to remember we were actually living in the twentieth century. As we crossed the estuary, which separated County Clare and County Kerry, it seemed we had stepped back one hundred years in time although the cottage was only a short distance from Shannon Airport. We arrived at the cottage early enough to buy groceries at the village shop. We asked for milk and received it "fresh from the coo". . . and in, yes, a whiskey bottle. There were no other containers; this was the standard for any liquid "to go."

The Atlantic laps gently at the beach at Carragahault, but a mile down the strand the sea pounds angrily against "One-Eye McMahon's" breakwater. (One-Eye, if the reader hasn't guessed already, was a pirate, with a vision problem left over from a resisted ship looting.)

The massive stone wall protects the robber chieftain's castle. The fortress is built on a long finger of land pushing back at the estuary. McMahon used the castle for a base to prey on local commerce and the occasional foreign sailing ship from France and Spain. At low tide we discovered the cave where he stored his contraband in the 1600s.

Two days after the wedding, Scott arranged a grand tour for the wedding party. A native Irishman drove us in his van. Down the coast from "One-Eye McMahon's" lair, we stopped to view the Cliffs of Mohar where the mighty Atlantic dashes its full force against the monumental stone structures carved by nature. A nearby pub boasts that it is "The last stop before Boston."

We saw a tiny island, isolated completely in the bay near Mohar's cliffs. The rocky speck of land, cut off completely, was covered with grass so green we could almost smell the minty freshness of it. In the spring, sheep are carried there by ship and lowered by pulleys to the isolated grass-covered rock to graze all summer! The rich grass nourishes the sheep, producing wool, which makes up the most sought-after sweaters in the world. Since Ireland's "Western World" is composed mostly of churches, still intact, and abbeys and ancient cathedrals, still in ruins—absolutely devastated since the 1600s when Cromwell and his forces swept through Ireland like a plague, destroying everything of value in their path, including cemeteries, and pubs—we were treated to an interesting exhibition. Our driver, probably one who had finally taken *the pledge*, made the sign of the cross while passing each holy place and pub! To our great anxiety, his hands were off the wheel more than on.

In some villages the pubs, churches, and cemeteries came so close together that we wondered if he was ever going to get his hands back on the wheel.

At a construction sight, there was a young lad trying to direct traffic. He held up a sign in the front which said SLOW. The other side said GO! Along the way were occasional signs alerting us to the dangers of "loose chippings."

The driver was oblivious to all warning signs and drove at breakneck speed on what seemed to us the "wrong" side of the road. Before long we suggested stopping someplace for lunch. We stopped in the village of Killkee at a family pub. School had just let out, and we were served both sandwiches and ale by a young lad. To most of our questions, he answered, "I haven't the slightest. . . ." But when asked if he wasn't a little young to be serving up drinks, he replied, "But I'm all of nine years, Mum!"

In western Ireland when a native asks the size of a village, he doesn't say, "How many people?" but always he asks, "How many pubs?"

The people of the "Western World" are unique. Past generations clung to their religion even more staunchly than most of us realized. During the centuries of religious persecution by the English overlords, they were denied land on which to build their churches after Cromwell laid waste their ancient cathedrals and simple village churches.

These steadfast Catholics had constructed a portable wooden chapel, which they dragged into the sea at the spot where the Atlantic first touches Ireland. The faithful heard

Mass barefoot, kneeling and standing in the waves, which crashed against the little chapel holding their priest. The men would then haul it to another spot. When the English authorities got wind of it and complained, the Irish replied, "Ye English may hold our land, but God still owns the Sea!"

We saw a simple stone chapel built in the present century, which houses and preserves the old wooden portable church.

Among the simple pleasures we enjoyed during our stay was getting to know the people near the village of Carragahault. They are not only the friendliest folk in the world but have preserved their pride and sense of humor intact through all the years of poverty and persecution.

One afternoon we saw a load of hay making its way slowly down a country road. On coming closer we saw an old man's legs protruding from the hay. He turned and smiled at us as we passed.

Another day a charming old man came out of his tumbledown cottage near McMahon's castle. He came out to speak to Rosemary, Annie, and me when he saw us pause by his stone fence.

"I'm an old pensioner, ye know," he began. "I travel all over de countryside on me bicycle dere." He indicated an ancient two-wheeler placed carefully against his doorstep. "It's all I need. I never could afford to marry; I fought all over the world with the British army. And now I've retired here with me pension."

In reply came the question, "Where were you born?" he said, "Here, in County Clare. But I'm really French, ye know. Me ancestor was a Norman French knight, De Roche he was. He came over with Strongbow, ye know," His eyes as well as his laughter sparkled as he added, "That was a few years ago . . . about eight hundred to be exact. But I still consider meself French."

The last night of our visit we saw many old bachelors at the village pub. Like us, they had come down for a glass of ale and a game of pool. It was the place we had bought our milk-in-a-whiskey-bottle that first afternoon.

After songs, jokes, and a few games of pool, which we lost to the Irish lads—perhaps due to their Irish style of playing and prediliction for "Irish Rules"—we were all invited by the local constable to get back to our cottages.

"Ye're breaking curfew," he said.

What time was it? All of nine o'clock.

I asked for some fresh milk to take back to the cottage for breakfast in the morning. The innkeeper was very surprised at my request.

"Are ye daft, missus?" he asked. "There is no milk now! The coos are thry! There'll be no more milk 'til the moooorning!"

That same day Scottie had finally remembered to return some fishing poles due back to a local merchant. He had rented them from a shop in Tralee, so he and Dudley Tom could go fishing. But first the owner had struck a bargain with Scottie.

"That will be a pound a day for each of ye until the poles are returned."

The men had meager luck on the streams, and Scottie forgot to return the poles. On this last day he sheepishly approached the shopkeeper and handed over the fishing equipment. The businessman looked sternly at our son-in-law, "Well, Laddie, at last ye remembered to bring the poles back. Do ye remember our bargain?"

"Indeed I do," said Scottie, "I'm afraid I owe you plenty."

"Well, now, Laddie, dunna worry sa much. How many fish de ye and yere faather-in-law actually catch?"

"I caught one and the same for my father-in-law from America."

"Now, that will be two pounds since ye actually caught only two fish." He smiled as he put the poles up on the dusty old rack with their brothers. "Does that sound fair to ye?"

Only in Ireland!

All too soon, the honeymoon week was over and we were back at Shannon Airport saying our good-byes.

When would we see our daughter again? We hugged and kissed our darling Rosemary and left her crying aloud, her whole body wracked with her sobs. Annie and I were crying, too as we walked toward the jetway and Tom had tears streaming down his cheeks. Kay stayed an extra day to make the final separation easier.

When would we see Rosemary again? Not soon. Our hearts would be in Ireland for eight more years until she returned to America permanently. She and Scott and their three children are now happily at home in a fairy-tale cottage in Connecticut.

Rosemary and Scott O'Carroll, Mr. and Mrs. O'Carroll, along with Tom and Patricia celebrating a wedding in Ireland circa 1979.

Batlands

(Or the Diary of a Bat-Mad Housewife)

AUGUST 3—Last summer a bat committed suicide in our house. It flew into a window fan in my beautiful blue bedroom. Early this summer I heard faint rustlings in the blue bedroom closet. Our daughter Annie, husband Rob, and their two daughters came for a visit in June. Anne, Rob, and their tiny baby Katie slept in the blue room with no dire consequences or visitations from bats, birds, etc., so I thought it would be safe for me to take up residence there again. So I'm sleeping upstairs again.

AUGUST 4—Last night I heard a scraping noise or maybe a bumping, grinding noise—bats entertaining themselves in my closet hiding behind Anne's wedding presents of three years' residence? I convinced myself it was merely our summer boarder, the dog Rufus, a handsome huge black Labrador Retriever whose dog house is directly beneath my bedroom windows. He must be scraping and chewing his dog house—or—*was it a bat in the closet, chowing down on the wedding gifts?*

AUGUST 6—It is now three nights after the scraping noise. I was trying to put myself to sleep by reading when some unidentified flying object dive-bombed my position, hurling itself at my head. It was a bat! Evidently its radar was down, and it didn't know I was there. I tried to scream for my husband Dudley Tom, who was downstairs. But only little squeaks emerged from my trembling, yet almost paralyzed vocal cords. Would-be screams sounded more like some wild trapped animal's dying effort.

Paralyzed as my vocal cords were, my limbs sprang into action and I flew down the stairs with the bat in hot pursuit—or so I thought.

Dudley Tom came to my rescue as fast as possible (not very fast, as he was having chest pains). He saw the little creature still flying around upstairs. I handed him a fish net (which hadn't worked on last year's bat) and a badminton racket.

He said, "I'm not going to kill that poor creature—we'll have to lure it outside some way!" He said this after slamming the bedroom door, imprisoning the poor thing in the blue bedroom.

Desperate for practical advice, I telephoned a Doctor of Veterinary Medicine. He said, "Don't worry, in a few weeks, it will migrate South; all bats migrate when it gets really cold."

I'm sure!

Why would our bat want to fly South when it could hang out in my nice warm closet and play hide-and-seek among the wedding presents?

AUGUST 7—This morning I called the Animal Control Department of our community to help with my bat problem. The man assigned to my call said, "Ma'am, I'm only in charge of getting rid of bees."

"No bats?" I asked.

"No," he answered.

"But what am I supposed to do?" I demanded.

"Lady, open a window in your bedroom, take out the screen, and let the bat fly out."

"But I don't know where the bat *is* now, and even if it does not come out of hiding and fly away, how do I know it won't fly back in? Along with birds, bees, wasps and flies?"

"Sorry I can't help you, Ma'am." he said through an audible grin. And that was that.

In the meantime Dudley Tom's chest pains have been diagnosed as gall bladder problems or pancreatitis. A heart attack has been ruled out thanks to an E.K.G.

AUGUST 8—I've tried to put the batlands (our upstairs) out of my mind. I've been sleeping on the very uncomfortable pullout couch the last two nights, but my dreams are all nightmares. Really weird ones with soldiers in black uniforms, hundreds of them, trussed together . . . *with bats in charge!*

I invaded the upstairs batlands today. I wore Dudley's camouflage fishin' hat with the protective veil covering my face. My appearance alone should have caused the bat to have a heart attack if he ventured forth and we met on the stairs, hall, or bedroom. I went upstairs to make my bed. I made it up in one second flat and then tore downstairs again. I hope I didn't make it up *with the bat in the bed.*

AUGUST 10—The first chapter of this Batlands Tale was brought to a tragic close (for the bat) this afternoon when my daughter Bridget's friend Jeanine ran upstairs to use the john. I didn't have the nerve to tell her we might have a bat in our bedroom, and certainly not that she might meet our bat on the stairs or hall. But I should have. In a moment we could hear her screams, and a second later she ran downstairs and yelled: "I thought somebody had forgotten to flush. *Probably a giant!* Then I looked again and saw it was—I couldn't believe it—*a dead bat in the toilet!*"

My daughter Bridget, who is a farmerette, very brave and strong of stomach, took care of the situation.

The poor creature, who was probably only trying to quench its thirst, drowned, and was disposed of thanks to Sir Thomas Crapper's invention. Maybe I can sleep tonight with no nightmares. (But I doubt if it will be in the blue room. That winged cousin of the squirrel may have siblings. Or in-laws.)

AUGUST 12—Today I heard some rustlings and scratchings, and little bat-type noises through the fireplace in the living room. Probably coming from the chimney. I hope it's only my imagination. . . .

AUGUST 14—Tonight as I was watching Public TV in the den, I happened to glance into the living room and my heart stopped! There were *two bats* swooping and gliding around. I yelled for Dudley. "*Please* close the fireplace damper!" I wailed. "Please open the front door and let them out!"

Through knitted fingers, covering my face in terror, I glimpsed Dudley in action. He was involved in a sort of minuet with the bats—advancing and retreating in a dance-like movement while he shook a fly swatter at them and urged them to fly out the front door. I didn't wait to see if the maneuver worked. I fled to the bathroom and locked the door. It was a while before I ventured out of the bathroom. *I'm going to sleep downstairs in the rose bedroom tonight. Dudley is strong and kinda fat and very brave and will surely intimidate any bats who are still lurking about upstairs.*

AUGUST 15—I called many Animal Control and Pest Control advertisers from the Yellow Pages. They all said, "We don't deal with bats!"

Finally I was referred to the one company in the Metro area brave enough to handle bats. All the while, Dudley kept commenting, "Why are you trying to get rid of the bats?

They're probably an endangered species—they get rid of insects."

I yelled back. "Endangered species? . . . *I've* lost five pounds worrying over this bat thing. *I'm* a nervous wreck!"

I contacted the *Great Bat Control Company*, and in due course, the batman arrived in his batmobile, after looking for an hour for our street. Some wild driver had thoughtlessly knocked down our street sign last night. Batman turned out to be kind, efficient and thorough. But bat-bravery aside, he had a bit of dog-phobia. He requested we confine our summer boarder, the handsome Lab Rufus, to the basement while he checked possible places of hideouts and hangouts inside our house. After donning heavy jacket and equipping himself with an electric brad (bats can sometimes be rabid—not usually, but our hero wanted all the odds on his side), he peeked and poked into closets and attic. He shinnied under a four-poster bed in the lavender room to check out a square hole my sons had cut in the wallboard to do plumbing repairs. He looked for droppings and sniffed for an unmentionable odor. No such things were found.

"I see no signs of signs of infestation inside," he commented, "but could I please have a glass of cold water?" Perspiration was rolling down his face, so I fetched him water then and soda pop. I repeated the libation several times later on during his ordeal, so perspiry was his exertion. Finally the nice batman went outside again and remarked, "Maybe the bats came through the fireplace before your husband closed the damper or through those vents at the peaks of your roof," pointing to one of them.

Remembering something useful, I said, "There's an old extension ladder next to the woodpile in the back yard. Maybe you could put that together and check out the vents to see if the screens are still in place."

"Okay!" he said.

But there was a tree growing through the ladder.

It had been in the same spot for at least ten years.

Stymied? Not our batman! He was not only nice but resourceful. He got our gas-powered saw, started it up, and proceeded to cut down the tree. Then he assembled the ladder after dragging it to the south facade, which led to the peak.

"Oh, oh!" I said. "One of the rungs is kinda rotten, I'd hate for you to climb this thing and fall and kill yourself."

"I'd hate that too," he said, sweat running down his face. Seeing his fatigue, I gave him yet another glass of pop.

Thwarted only momentarily, my desperation spawned an idea.

"Why don't you just *look* through Dudley's *binoculars* and see from the ground if the vents still have protective screens on them? Then you won't have to take the chance of falling from that old ladder."

Archimedes couldn't have been more proud of his bathtub act with Pericles's crown than I when the idea worked!

Look, he did; and luck we had. Screens still intact.

Batman was so nice that he did not charge for his lumberjack work. What's more, he gave us a fifteen percent discount because we are senior citizens. He left with this reassuring message: "Call me immediately if you see any more bats!"

Saying that, he sounded more like a bat doctor than a bat batter.

We waved good-bye to him, and he took off in his batmobile.

AUGUST 16—Two little granddaughters spent the night tonight on the pullout couch in the living room with no more bat alarms. All is quiet on the Kavanagh front. Now if our luck will hold until October 31. . . .

P.S. To diary peekers: Should the reader, with Halloween fast approaching, feel the need of my <u>now expert</u> batalogic, or an introduction to our very own batman, call me at 1-800-BATLADY. (Just kidding!)

ABOUT THE AUTHOR—Some wish to say Pat Kavanaugh is Redford's answer to Erma Bombeck. This editor feels Pat is a little too individual to be easily compared . . . except maybe to Samuel Clemens, had Huck and Tom's narrator been born a woman. To this observer Pat is a little less sanguine, a little more ruminative, and a lot more "I'm from Missouri, so show me your rocket before I buy stock in your trip to the moon." Though the former Miss Blanton was reared in St. Louis in the 30s and 40s, this editor finds her skepticism (and caution) having much local and current (Halloween is coming!) appeal—we Michigan natives may not be an endangered species, but we're aware perils hereabouts are not limited to out-of-state-transplants. In other words Pat's diary notations will strike a responsive chord with most of us. What's more we may learn a lesson or two, based on her "bat-out-of-hell investigations."—FEB

Cabin Calls

Kayme and I had been on board and in our cabin for less than ten minutes, and already someone was knocking gently but firmly on our cabin door. Like the friend of Barnacle Bill, I asked, "Who's that knocking at my door?"

"It's only me, it's nobodyeeeee," was the soft-spoken reply.

I flung open the door to find our cabin boy Joseph. He told us he was a native of Jamaica, as were most of the service personnel on our cruise.

"I'm here to serve you, Madame and Missy," he said in his beautiful Caribbean patois, nodding first to me and then to my young daughter.

It was the first of many encounters with the crew and passengers that Kayme and I were to have during a week-long cruise through the Caribbean with ports-of-call at Cap-Haitin, San Juan, St. Thomas, and Nassau.

I had been ill with a serious case of double pneumonia. To speed my recovery, my father had treated me to this trip away from the turmoil and pressures that always accompany life with a big family. I had asked my second daughter, Kayme, to join me since she had never been out of the States while the other two older girls had traveled widely.

I thought travel with Kayme would be soothing since she was more conservative and straight while the other two fancied themselves radicals. I should have remembered that while Kayme didn't cause excitement exactly, she seemed to attract it.

For instance, her two sisters had come to Washington, D.C., for the '71 Peace Protest. Deda flew from the south of France and Reenie, the ultra radical of the family, hitchhiked with co-conspirators from Michigan State University.

Kayme, who lived and worked in D.C., did not take part in the protest but was the only one of the trio who was tear-gassed. That happened when she was trying to enter the office building where she worked, supposedly protected by her boss who nearly passed out from the gas.

But, getting back to my story, later on during the first night of our cruise, I had been awakened about 2:00 A.M. by Kayme's sobbing and moaning.

"What's the matter, honey?" I asked in sympathy.

"Oh, Mother, I have the most terrible pains all over my abdomen! I don't think I can stand it any longer. It's been hurting for hours, but I didn't want to wake you. Ooooohhh, Oooohhh!"

I decided right then and there to call the ship's doctor for help. I had visions of an appendix getting ready to burst with the closest hospital a few hundred nautical miles on the other side of a hurricane. We had heard through the grapevine that we were skirting the fringes of a newly born and ever-strengthening hurricane. We were told later by a young member of a ship's staff that we should not be alarmed if the ship began to toss and sway during the night.

All these thoughts raced through my mind as I tried first to make myself understood by the switchboard operator who was either Norwegian or Jamaican but obviously speaking and understanding some language I did not share with him. Secondly, when I was finally connected to the doctor by ship's phone, I discovered that he was definitely Spanish and although he understood English and comprehended that I wanted him to come immediately, please, to my cabin because my daughter was seriously ill, I did not understand too well his answer to me,

"It's two in ze night. Who's to get zick at two in ze night?"

"My twenty-one-year-old daughter. I think she may have appendicitis!"

"Oh, you're ze mama? Appendicitis! Terrible, terrible! I come right away! Please to give me number of ze cabin."

The doctor appeared in about five minutes flat, his white jacket buttoned askew but with reassuring, black bag which means help is at hand in any language.

"This is twenty-one-year-old senorita? Looks more like litta twelve-year-old girs to me, and you don' look like no mama!"

With this opening greeting, he sat down on the bed next to Kayme and began to examine her. Then he shouted at me, "Lights, more lights! Please, Mama! Give me more lights! Please to turn on light over litta girs' bed!"

In my panic and eagerness to help, I punched the light switch again, immediately throwing the tiny cabin into total darkness. The doctor responded with some wild medicated Spanish oath while his cold clammy hands kept probing the hot inflamed abdomen of my terror-stricken daughter. Her moans became a low background accompaniment for the loud sharp staccato of his exclamations. I quickly punched the correct light switch.

"Eet look more like spastic colon. I geeve you suppositories for heer to take. Weel calm heer down eenside. Now I geeve to heer ze injection to make heer relax and sleep. Don' look like appendicitis to me! But if pain keep up or come back, we take litta girs to mine friend's hospital when we get to Haiti day after tomorra. Zat weel be fifteen dollar, pleez!"

The next day, Sunday, Doctor Juanez made two more cabin calls to check on Kayme's condition. These two calls were unsolicited and unwanted, although we appreciated his interest and concern. She had recovered overnight. You see, according to ship's regulations, which we had studied carefully, the doctor was allowed to charge fifteen dollars for each cabin call. He hadn't presented us with bills for the second and third cabin calls at the time.

We lived in constant terror that the doc *would* present these bills at any moment. At fifteen bucks a call, that would have totaled forty-five, a drastic reduction of our small funds to spend on the trip.

Together we had the grand total of only one hundred dollars. Out of that we had to tip the cabin boys, the dining-room waiters, and maitre d', plus buy presents for my enormous family (one husband and ten children who hadn't gone on the trip.) So you can see why we weren't anxious to pay Doc Juanez for the two visits we hadn't even requested.

The rest of the trip we spent in studiously avoiding him, so he wouldn't ask us for the thirty bucks. Sometimes we avoided him subtly, like hiding behind the huge potted palms of the Tropicana Nightclub on the sundeck, or under our table in the dining room when we saw him coming our way.

Sometimes we had to avoid him more strenuously like the time Kayme and I were swimming in the puddle-sized swimming pool on the top deck. I looked up after rounding the width of the pool via the backstroke, and there was the Doc screaming at me, "Mama, why you and litta girs alway hide from me? You afraid of me or sometheeeng?"

I was so surprised I gulped a couple of mouthfuls of briny sea water from the tiny pool before diving beneath the surface again. I wasn't afraid of him, but I was afraid of that thirty-dollar bill, which I was sure he was going to serve me with.

The next time we ran into the Doc, I was in a public phone booth in the central square of the old district of San Juan. I was trying to talk to an old college friend, a native of

San Juan; I was able to speak to him in English since he had been educated in the States. It was hard for me to carry on a conversation with him, though.

All the buses traveling through San Juan to Santurce and the Contado District seemed to originate at that square and at that moment. The din was overpowering. My old friend was interrogating me, "What? You have eleven children? Impossible, but then you always did tell wild tales! Really, eleven? Did you bring all of them with you and your husband, too?"

My mind was doing fast arithmetic: thirteen times the horrible amount of money my father had spent on only my expenses. I began to laugh. I was sure I would never see that much money in my lifetime. My laughter soon turned to screams and I had to say a quick "Adios" and hang up on Emilio because someone was trying to beat me up. A huge derelict was pounding me on the back and screaming at me, "You have money for a telephone call, you have money to geeve me. You geeve me money, Senora!"

Kayme was yelling right back at my attacker and trying to drag him away from me, but he kept right on pummeling me. That's when Doc Juanez appeared, and for once we were glad to see him. He said something in Spanish to our tormenter who immediately slunk away.

"Ah, Mama and litta girs, for once it's good theeng you couldn't hide from me so good. I take you back to sheep now and you go with some more bodyeees nex time you go ashore."

We knew now that he had completely forgotten about the thirty dollars and we did, too.

Grosse Isle Homestead

Kay Corbett was one of my friends at Maryville College of the Sacred Heart in my hometown of St. Louis, Missouri. We were in the same Shakespeare and art studio classes during World War II. When the war was finally over and my handsome Air Force captain husband and I were established in Detroit, I telephoned Kay. She was living with her parents, Syd and Lucy Corbett, on Grosse Isle, a very special island residential enclave in the Detroit River.

Syd and Lucy wrote a charming column called *Pot Shots from a Grosse Isle Kitchen* for the *Detroit News* Sunday Woman's Section. Their writing, a combination of lively anecdotes and mouth-watering gourmet recipe format, had quickly become one of the most popular items in the *News* Sunday edition.

Tom and I and baby Maureen were privileged to be invited to dinner many times at the Corbetts' island home.

Lucy, Kay, and I had similar interests—literature, drama, and art as well as the usual feminine domestic concerns. Syd, who had become partially paralyzed and trapped in a wheelchair, shared like backgrounds with Tom. They both had seen overseas wartime duty, Syd in World War I and Tom in World War II. They both loved to read and hunt and fish. They regaled each other with bigger and bigger tales of prowess in the field or on the water. And they often discussed the possible location and destiny of the homestead and farm where Tom's great-grandfather, James Kavanagh, had lived in the pioneer days and early settlement of the island.

One evening as they talked, Syd showed Tom his favorite old shotgun, which wasn't operating properly. Tom took the precious old firearm apart, corrected the problem, and handed it back to Syd.

Kay's bedroom was a huge affair, with an attractive four-poster bed and a wallpaper with graceful sprays of soft green ivy wandering all over it in a fanciful painted design. I loved going up there to share private conversations. But the first time I climbed the stairs, I was a bit perturbed. I was born with a fear of heights, and this staircase went on and on and on and on. It was a beautiful fairytale thing, a winding circular affair with no visible support. Kay said legend had it that the staircase was brought over by sailing ships long ago from England. The thing was very shaky, and so was I by the time I reached the second floor.

Kay laughed and said, "You can go down by the back stairs when we're ready. They're safe and solid."

This was no problem. I was used to the front stairs-back stairs set-up. That's the way my grandparents' home in Bay City and my parents' home in southeast Missouri were arranged. In the Missouri house, the only time the servants were allowed to use the front stairs was when they were cleaning them.

We lost touch with the Corbetts through the years of a growing family and pressing business matters with all their demands, although I kept a copy of Syd and Lucy's book *Long Windows* at my bedside and often reread parts of it when I needed a comforting homey support in trying times.

Two summers ago, at one of Tom's cousin's seventieth birthday party, we saw another cousin from the Kavanagh side of the family. He paused at our table and said, "Guess what? I was looking up some old tax records for a client and came across our great-grandfather's name. The first time he paid taxes on Grosse Isle was in 1842. I have the address of the property, too, so if you ever have time to come down to the island, you could see where your great-grandpappy lived. In fact, the old Kavanagh house is the background for the new Buick Roadmaster commercial on TV so watch for it. Of course, new wings have been added to the old homestead through the years, so it doesn't look the same as when the Kavanaghs lived there, but it will be fun for you to see it."

We did watch for the commercial and saw it many times. The house looked like a beautiful old mansion.

Our oldest daughter, Maureen, came soon for a visit. She's an attorney living in Virginia now. She has represented the government in historical preservation litigation. We thought she might be interested in seeing the old place. She was eager to go with us to the island. I called Tom's cousin's house, and his wife gave us the phone number and address of the present owner.

It took me an entire thirty minutes to work up the courage to call the owner of the old house, but when I did reach her, she was very gracious. I asked her if we could come over and just take pictures of the outside of the house.

"I'm leaving at 1:30 tomorrow afternoon for my son's wedding in Chicago," she said, "but you're certainly welcome to stand outside the house and take pictures."

I was so excited for my husband. For years he had wanted to find out just where the old farm was, and now we were actually going to see it. I was excited, too, for myself, because I love old houses, especially those connected with our families.

I noticed that the address was on the same road as the old Corbett house and thought they might possibly be in the same neighborhood. We drove down river and crossed the Detroit River from Trenton on the toll bridge.

It was a beautiful day. The river was busy with ships from many foreign countries. The island itself looked lovely, with its big old residences, spacious green lawns, edged with colorful flowerbeds and majestic old trees. We were so busy looking first at the river and then the homes, like someone at a tennis match, that we went past the address.

Tom turned the car around and we came back along East River Road very slowly, closely examining each number on each mailbox.

Maureen said, "Well, this is the right name and number—right here!" I looked up at the house across the wide expanse of lawn and said, "There must be some mistake. This doesn't look like the house in the commercial. Why—this is the old house the Corbetts lived in when we used to visit them almost fifty years ago!"

Tom exclaimed as he was continuing down the long driveway past the side of the house, "It's the right house. See—the back has been added to. With all these wings added on, this is the view we saw on the TV commercial!"

We couldn't believe it. We both laughed out loud. He said, "Remember when we used to sit at the table eating dinner with the Corbetts, and Syd and I would conjecture where the old Kavanagh house could be and we were right *in* it!"

I said to Maureen, "You used to come here with us when you were a baby."

Tom had pulled into the parking area by the back door. We were so flabbergasted by the situation that I hesitated knocking on the door to let the owner know who we were.

"I'll go up to the door with you," Maureen said.

We gathered our courage and approached the door. The owner had seen us coming and greeted us very politely. I reckon she thought we looked trustworthy because she said, "You're welcome to come inside if you'd like to."

I beckoned to Tom, who was already getting out of the car with a big grin on his face.

"You won't believe this," I said to the gracious lady, "but we used to visit this house many years ago when the Corbetts lived here. We wondered at the time where Tom's ancestors' homestead was, and we were sitting right in it!"

She laughed, too, and showed us the interior. It looked beautiful, both the original front area where Tom's ancestors had lived as well as the newer additions. She is an excellent decorator and every room is charming.

I pointed out the graceful old winding staircase, still dancing its way to the second floor.

"I used to be afraid to climb that thing because it was so shaky," I said, "and Kay would let me use the back stairs."

Our hostess said as she directed our attention to the huge and very unusual old double doors at the side entry of the original portion, "Those doors were from the old fort, which guarded the island during the War of 1812. It was near the location of this house."

After we took photographs both inside and out, we were on our way. We thanked our gracious hostess, who was leaving for her son's wedding. I was so excited over our happy adventure I was afraid I wouldn't be able to sleep that night. But I did sleep and well. The fresh air and sunshine and happiness of the day relaxed us all. My darling Tom had found or rather *refound* the old Kavanagh homestead at last.

Tom and Reenie in front of the Grosse Isle Homestead. The door behind them was taken from the fort that guarded the island in the War of 1812.

People Ask

I

People ask why I've never written about my mother. "You've written poems and stories about your father, Grandmother, great-greats—why nothing about your mother?" Who could write about his mother? I can't—it would be like cutting through Everest or preserving a soap-bubble. Mothers are for loving, not explaining. How explain an ivory skin and great brown eyes, dreamy eyes the color of hot fudge sauce. That was her favorite vice—sneaking a hot-fudge sundae when she thought she was overweight or really couldn't afford it, because after all, she had eight children and she always saw to their needs first. When she was angry or disapproved of what my father or one of us had done, her eyes turned hard and cold and purple-black like the royal robe she didn't need to wear to prove she was a queen. One stern look from her was more scathing than a lash and hurt far worse. Although she had spanked us and spanked us hard when she thought we needed it to get us through "the Ornery age," which was any age that seemed to make us ornery.

II

Her mouth was beautifully shaped, full and sensuous, but she didn't even know how to flirt, so she said it was wasted on her. She said she never could learn to wink successfully and it would have come in handy when she attended Balls and Hops at the Naval Academy at Annapolis. She was a student at Trinity College in D.C. and was more interested in organizing midnight feasts and suffragette marches than setting her Edwardian cap for a midshipman or the Georgetown student who eventually became my father. She was invited to a reception at the White House where she was questioned by Secret Service agents because she had gone through the receiving line three times. She explained to them she was merely checking—she was wearing a supposedly exclusive designer's dress and the President's daughter, in the receiving line, had on an exact copy.

III

She loved to ride horseback when she was a young girl and once rode a horse that ran away with her for twenty miles, but instead of being afraid, she loved it and laughed hilariously all the way, partially at the efforts of her Philosophy professor, Doctor Ryan, who was trying to keep up with her, riding an old nag.

IV

She put the same zest into rearing her family; they all were university graduates, the four boys with doctorates in various fields. She had a beautiful voice, had studied voice and opera in New York, but preferred singing solo parts in her parish church choir to pursuing a stage career. Her four girls had piano lessons for eight years. It was wasted on me—I've no talent, but I did learn the cross-over method of playing, which I found useful when I taught myself to type. I remember her taking me into her bed one morning to diagram twenty sentences. It was five o'clock and she had to feed the baby at six. When I got to school, Sister Felicatis apologized for assigning the wrong page—we wouldn't start diagramming till the Spring—I was the only one whose mother had done her homework. Nothing was too much to do for her children or anyone lonesome or in need—a neighbor or stranger. The Me-firsters and "look Out for No. One-ers" would never have understood.

V

She had a stroke when she was seventy and for seven years she was locked in her body, her beautiful right hand now a cold claw, twisted and useless. When she could move about again, it was with help and she dragged her right leg behind her.

VI

The night before she died, she had a dream, which she told the next day to her faithful servant who had worked for her forty years. She dreamed that she was a young girl again, riding horseback with her long black hair streaming in the wind. She rode for a while, then dismounted and ran lightly and gracefully through flowered meadows of the most beautiful country she had ever seen.

VII

The day of her funeral was bitter and cold. The night before when I had slept in her deserted bed, an icy wind rattled the shutters, moaned at the weather stripping and wailed down the chimney of the old house like a banshee crying, "Maureeeeen, Maureeeeen!" It was the first day of Spring in Missouri. Usually jonquils, tulips and Japanese quince would have bloomed, but that year the ground was still frozen at the graveyard and cold rain and wind mocked the mourners as we gathered around the grave. I had been strong until the metal lid was fastened over the rosewood coffin, trapping my mother forever. She could never get out now. I shivered and heard my daughter sob, "Grandma!" Deep inside me, my heart screamed, "Mother!"

VIII

She left all her best china to me, and to one of my sons her diamond ring for his bride to wear someday when he grew up. Because he had always been so kind to her, the first to help her walk and move in and out of cars. Mothers are for loving, not explaining. That's what I say when people ask. When they ask why I never write about my mother.

Annapolis Drag

First we lit the giant firecrackers and threw them down the large opening known as "The Well." A second later when we saw that they had streaked past the third and second floors and were sure to explode as they reached the marble entrance hall, Ann and I each threw our small round torpedoes with all our seventeen-year-old strength.

Bang, bang, bang, bam, bam, slam, slam, BAAAANG! BAAAAANG! went our fireworks! We started for our dorm room, intending to hide under our beds. But I decided that was stupid. "No, Ann," I whispered, "we should rush back to the well and look surprised and scared like everyone else is!" We ran back and peered over our fourth-floor railings in time to hear poor old Mrs. Thuey yell down the well, "Are ye alive or dead?" Thuey was the night patroller.

"I think I'm alive!" the night watchman yelled back to Thuey, and all of us girls hanging over the great opening.

"What is it? What's the matter? Are the Germans bombing us already? They haven't declared war on us yet, have they?" Dozens of girlish voices were screaming at each other, and Mrs. Thuey.

Most of the nuns were sleeping in the cloistered section of Trinity College and were not able to survey the situation immediately.

"Seems to be no damage down here," the night watchman yelled up to Thuey. "Get those silly girls back to bed!"

Mrs. Thuey, one of two large elderly chaperones, whose duty it was to patrol the halls endlessly all night long, shooed us all back to our rooms. My roommate, Ann, and I knew we were bored most of the time at our all-girls private Catholic college in Washington, D.C. and figured the night chaperones must be ten times as bored as we were. It was *our* duty to give them something exciting to cope with occasionally. Keep them on their toes. Let them earn their money. Otherwise they would have nothing more exciting to do than search with flashlights for nonexistent men who never got smuggled into the dorm. They needed flashlights to see their way up and down the long halls, the great staircases, the nooks and crannies and the bathrooms because *all* the lights in the main building were turned off at nine o'clock by a master switch on weekdays. The young ladies must have their proper rest. Anyone who hadn't crammed sufficiently for finals or semi-finals resorted to studying by flashlight under heavy bedcovers or in the bathtubs. Towels were hung over transoms and stuffed under doors to camouflage our strategy. An ongoing battle of wits with the system, which insisted on treating grown women like us as children.

If they treated us like children, we would act like real children. Some nights we roller-skated from midnight till one A.M. down jet-black halls, confounding our enemies, the night patrollers. They couldn't figure out why those thunder noises were heard only *inside* the building or who or what was making them.

It was autumn of 1939. Germany had invaded Poland. England and France were now at war with her, too. How long before we got into it? And here we were going to school in D.C., the nation's capital.

My older sister Rosemary and I were attending the same college that our mother had graduated from in 1916. A family tradition. Rosemary was a sophomore and I was a freshman. Only we weren't going to stay the four years till graduation. Thank God for small favors. It wasn't that I hated Trinity or anything like that. I really *loved* it. And the girls. And most of the teachers.

I especially loved the Biology nun. She was a world-famous scientist who had entered the nun factory after her husband had died and her children reared. She was definitely a human being. She could see that I weighed only eighty-five pounds and needed every last minute of R.E.M. I could squeeze out of my fragile brain. Especially after a night of general hell-raising, like the night of the fireworks episode.

She had a roll call every morning at the beginning of class. Although my last name was Blanton and should have been called with the B's, this darling nun called my name after the Z's. There were forty-three in this section of her Biology class. She called my name forty-third because otherwise I would have to get late marks on my reports sent home to my anxious parents in St. Louis. Ann and I waited till the eight-twenty-five warning bell before we even opened our eyes if we had an eight-thirty class. Then a regular tornado of activity—we pulled on the round garters, which held up our pajama legs and threw on our raincoats as we raced for our class. Luckily the classrooms were in the same building. And lucky we were that we didn't get graded on our appearance for that first class, either.

Yes, I really did love everything about Trinity except their darn smothering *rules!* The board of directors were living in the 1800s, not the twentieth century. It was Mother's spoken wish that all of her daughters would enjoy at least one year at her alma mater. The most prestigious Catholic girls' college in the U.S. Of course, Manhattanville and Maryville thought *they* were!

Mother's *unspoken* wishes for her daughters were for us to catch rich husbands from fine old families and for me finally to settle down and become a lady. Hopefully, we would take advantage of this marvelous opportunity to meet suitable husband material, and I would get over my penchant for highjinks that had driven the nuns wild at the high school we had attended in our suburb outside of St. Louis.

Our mother had met our father when she was a student at Trinity and he a law student at Georgetown. And our Grandma Blanton had met Grandpa when she was a business college student in D.C. and he a handsome young engraver at the Treasury Department. He had rented a room in one of Great-Grandma Cullen's townhouses conveniently located close to Georgetown Law School, which four of Grandma's brothers attended.

So you see it was definitely also a family tradition to meet and "catch" your husband in D.C. But how could we do that? Trinity had medieval dating rules. We girls felt trapped. We had to have something to look forward to, therefore the pranks. It seemed I'd *never* become a lady! These were their stupid rules:

Freshmen had to be back on campus and "signed in" by six o'clock every day, even on weekends. We were allowed one date a month! On this one date, we had to be in the main building and signed in by nine-thirty. At nine-thirty, all doors were locked. Any young lady who was locked out at nine-thirty was automatically expelled. She brought disgrace not only to herself but her family, her entire community, probably even to the whole state of Missouri.

How could I put up with this nonsense? Mother had never put a time limit on our coming in from dates at home. Her mother had been so strict with her that she went in the opposite direction. She was really empathetic. She didn't want her daughters getting that queasy feeling in our stomachs because we might be five minutes late.

So how could I put up with this stupid Trinity rule stuff? I had been going out on dates for years. Every night during holiday vacations and summers and every night of every weekend during the school year.

My mother even let her daughters have study dates during the week when we were in high school. The excuse was the need for extra assistance in Latin or Algebra or Geometry. Only *one* date a month? Holy Cow! How could I stand it?

There were two redeeming cracks in the rules at Trinity. The first allowed a student to go out any time with a member of her own family to spend whole weekends with a family member if he or she was visiting D.C. or happened to live in town. Sister Rosemary and I were very lucky in this category.

Our father was the Federal District Attorney for the eastern half of Missouri. He was often in town on official business. He sprang us from our prison to go out to dinner, even during the week. Uncle Milton from Atlanta was in D.C. occasionally, too, and treated us to dinner at O'Donnells, a prime sea-food restaurant. And joy of joys, our Aunt Catherine actually lived in Washington! She managed the office of Senator Pat Harrison of Mississippi. When we had been confined to the campus so long we felt we would go absolutely *mad*, either Rosemary or I would telephone Aunt Catherine. In spite of her busy job, she always came to our rescue. She would call Sister Angela, Dean of Women, and arrange for us and a couple of our Trinity friends to come to her apartment for the weekend. She set up dates for formal Mississippi state balls, Redskin football games, and sometimes just plain old relaxing dateless weekends with her alone. She was a doll.

The second redeeming break in the impossible dating rules at Trinity were the balls, tea dances, and mixers given at the Shoreham or Mayflower hotels, which we were allowed to attend if lucky enough to receive an invitation. The catch was that for the formal proms or balls, we Trinity girls had to go en masse on chartered buses and meet our Georgetown or Catholic U. dates at the ballroom! We were never allowed to go in a taxi or private car to one of these social affairs.

And before we were allowed on the bus, we gathered in the Trinity parlor and prayed with Sister Angela that our purity and/or virginity would be left intact by the time this evening of social contact, of cheek-to-cheek dancing with young men was over. It was impossible for us to lose anything at the balls, as we were allowed to leave the ballroom only to go to the powder room. There were chaperones located at strategic points to ensure we didn't leave the area.

So you see, although we did get out of the building occasionally, I never had the freedom to go to a university or college for a weekend, as my friends in Missouri did. Until my luck suddenly changed. Rosemary was invited to Annapolis for a Naval Academy weekend by an old friend from Missouri. Then she came down with the flu. Her bad luck was my good luck.

"How would you like to go to Annapolis in my place, Pat? I'm just too sick with this rotten flu." Her eyes were watering, and she was holding her head as she spoke. Silly question! I was *dying* to go!

Sister Angela gave permission for me to go to Annapolis in Rosemary's place. A few minutes before we boarded the bus, which carried the young ladies from Trinity to the Naval Academy, Sister Angela met privately with me and the senior who was to be my chaperone for the weekend.

"Now, you know we usually don't allow freshmen to go to men's colleges for the weekend. The only reason you're going is because this senior will be staying at the same house as you, so you'll be properly supervised. And we don't want that young man who may soon be fighting for his country to be disappointed."

The young man was Clay Mitchell. He was about four years older than I and probably didn't even remember me from grade-school days. I hoped I wouldn't bore him.

The senior and I boarded the chartered bus together. That was the last I saw of my so-called chaperone. She said, “I’ll see you Sunday night when we get on the bus to return to Trinity. There are no rooms available at my house. Clay and my date have found you a room at another approved home in Annapolis.”

Clay met me at the bus and took me to the house to drop off my luggage. I don’t think he was especially looking forward to “dragging” his old friend Rosemary’s younger sister for the weekend. In 1939 at Annapolis, a drag meant a date—not what it means today.

Clay was in an intermural wrestling match that weekend. He won his match. I had been cheering for him like mad. When I was a teenager, I loved going to wrestling matches. Probably a subconscious wish for a little body contact.

The “hop”was a formal ball that Saturday night. I had been worried for hours that the stag line might not cut in and poor Clay would be “stuck” with me. Every young girl’s nightmare in the thirties and forties. Not to worry. I had worn my prettiest gown. All Clay’s friends were curious to meet the substitute date. I got quite a rush. In fact, Clay became annoyed because he didn’t get to dance with me more than a few minutes before some other midshipman would cut in.

This happened all through the hop. One fellow in particular wouldn’t leave me alone. He kept cutting in every few minutes. His name was A.B.C. Fires. I was fascinated by his name. I had known plenty of boys with initials for names, such as G.B. Greer and G.C. Baker back home. But I had never met anyone before who advertised himself with *three* initials! How ridiculous!

Clay thought the situation was getting ridiculous, too. “Let’s sit this dance out, Pat. I really haven’t had a chance to say more than a few words to you all evening.” Clay led me to a comfortable couch in the adjoining parlor. “I’m so glad you came, Pat. You've cheered me up. I've been very depressed."

"Why—what's the matter?" I asked.

"I was engaged to this lovely girl back home. When I left for the Academy, I asked my best friend to keep an eye on her. To see that she didn't get too lonesome. Well, she wasn't lonesome for long."

"You mean she got a crush on him?"

"Much more than a crush. They started dating after a few months."

"Oh, I'm so sorry, Clay."

"But what really hurt was that neither one of them told me for a long time. They were married about a month ago. That's why I wanted a date for this weekend. Thank you for coming, Pat. The orchestra is playing our favorite song now. I don't want to hear it. Do you mind if we go back to your house now? The dance is about over, anyway."

"Fine with me, Clay," I answered.

The soft strains of the song followed us as we put on our cloaks: "The dearest things I know are what you are. You are the promised kiss of Springtime that makes the lonely winter seem blue, etc."

The words were so touching and I could imagine how they were hurting Clay now. It started to snow as we walked to the house and I began slipping and sliding in my four-inch dance shoes. Clay put an arm around me to steady me and soon we were at our destination. The living room was in darkness. It was filled with loving couples, most of them engaged to be married or about to be. There was one empty chair.

Clay and I latched on to it. We were both slight and I fitted quite comfortably on his lap. He was so lonely. He tried to kiss me, and of course I let him. Just a few sweet friendly kisses. Nothing passionate, nothing compromising. I knew my mother would think it the kind thing to do, too. Even Sister

Angela might approve. I didn't know what my best beau back in St. Louis would have thought about it, though. It was all for a patriotic cause, and what Billy didn't know wouldn't hurt him.

The next day, Sunday, Clay took me to see a movie, *Jamaica Inn.* After almost fifty years, I still remember the name. It was great. Suspenseful, exciting, and a wonderful windup for our weekend. On the way to the bus, the walking was really treacherous. The ground was as slippery as frozen white silk.

So I said to Clay, "As long as I'm your drag this weekend, you're goin' to have to *really* drag me. I can't walk one more step on these horrible high heels!"

I hung onto his arm and let him drag me to the bus that we could see a short distance away. As a parting shot, I suddenly stopped and scooped a handful of snow. I made a nice big snowball and aimed it at Midshipman A.B.C. Fires who was passing by. It hit him squarely on the back of his neck.

Clay laughed and said, "It's a good thing he's not an upper classman or I'd be in big trouble!" We kissed good-bye.

I never saw him again. Nor did my sister Rosemary. He was killed in a plane crash during the war on a routine flight for the Navy. But sometimes I hear the old song, "All the Things You Are" on nostalgic radio programs. And every time I hear it, I get tears in my eyes.

Romance of a Mud Dauber

For the fourth time that evening, I had answered the phone, only to hear a masculine voice say, "Hello, Pat, this is Joe—is Moe home?"

My sister Maureen (Moe) was in the curious and confusing situation of dating five boys named Joe simultaneously, not to mention numerous Bills, Bobs, Jacks, and one Smedley. Every time the voice at the other end of the line said, "This is Joe," I had to reply, "Which Joe?"

This immediately deflated the poor boy's ego but didn't discourage him from making another dozen calls to Moe every week.

When the phone rang for the fifth time, I grudgingly rose from the dinner table, thinking it would probably be the fifth Joe. Instead, a very feminine voice with Southern intonations and a slight suggestion of French asked, "Is that you, Pat dahling?"

I immediately recognized Mother Mouton's soft voice. She had called to invite me to attend a special summer school course in sculpture. Classes to be held in the large recreation room at Maryville College where I had finished my junior year.

"You can pay for the class by working in the library in the afternoons, helping Mother Dowling repair old books. The sculpture class will be only in the mornings before the day becomes too hot, while you still feel strong. Your teacher will be a lovely man—Ivan Schlitvisky. He's very charming and I'm sure you'll enjoy the class, dear. I've chosen a very select group. Each has outstanding artistic ability. It's all settled, dear? Then I'll see you at school on Monday next?"

What had I gotten myself into? Moe had already started work as an instructor in Phys Ed at a public playground near Maryville and was earning good money. I had planned to get a summer job, too, but as Mother wasn't too well that summer, I had been hesitant about leaving her without any helpers. This sculpture course sounded interesting but seemed frivolous compared with what Moe was doing.

Monday I awoke to the usual morning sounds of our home. The horrible war news was blaring forth from the radio downstairs. The scraping of the toast my mother had burned in the oven was an added irritant to my ears, which would rather have been listening to the people I had just left behind in my dreams.

According to the radio, Rommel was chasing the British all over North Africa, and I knew my mother was eloquently although inaudibly cursing the burnt toast. She was too much of a lady to ever actually say, "DAMN!" but she constantly muttered, "That D toast!" Or "That D oven" under her breath, so that the end result was the same. She felt relieved and the object of her scorn was thoroughly told off.

I remembered with a start what day it was. Moe and I both sprang out of bed, dressed, and went through the motions of eating breakfast to please Mother. Neither one of us could look an egg in the eye so early in the day. From that first day forward, I usually just grabbed a piece of Mother's burnt and scraped toast plus orange juice as I tore through the front door to the streetcar at the end of the block. I did stop for a moment to speak with Mrs. Maury, who lived next door. A flag with two stars hanging in her living-room window showed that two members of her household were serving their country.

One star was for her oldest son, Bobbie. The other was for their dog, Prince, who was doing his duty for God and country in the K-Nine Corps. I asked how Bobbie was. She told me, and then as an afterthought, I asked, "And what do you hear from Prince?" She merely looked at me and shook her head.

When I reached school and entered the rec room where the sculpture class was to be held, the instructor and three nuns were the only ones there. Mother Mouton introduced me. "This is Professor Schlitvisky, Pat dahling, and Mother Crump and Mother Watkins." Mother Crump was pleasingly plump and Mother Watkins tall and very dignified.

Professor Schlitvisky was disarmingly handsome. He was tall with broad shoulders, wavy brown hair. His eyes were warm and intelligent. They were a soft brown with flecks of gold. They seemed to light up and catch fire when he was especially pleased about something or confiding to us a past episode of his life in a low intimate tone or when he was trying to convert his pupils to his point of view on a wide variety of subjects.

I found out later that those broad shoulders of his disappeared when he took off his well-padded suitcoat and put on his working smock. A few days later, he admitted to us that he regularly had his hair "done" at a men's hair-styling shop. I never knew if the word "done" meant his hair was washed, dyed, waved or cut, or whether it wasn't really his own but a wig, which he left off at a shop to have restored regularly.

A well-shaped luxuriant mustache lent a sophisticated touch above his mouth, which was manly but full enough to belong to his sensuous, sensitive artist's face. His teeth were good, but not *too* good. I was sure they, at least, were his own.

The sculptor bowed slightly, and as he was asking me about my background in art, the other members of the class came in. I recognized Sally Brown. She was a senior at Maryville with an extraordinary face, despite her reputation as a genius in mathematics and creative writing. Her efforts at sculpture bore out my opinion of her. Adequate but not exciting. In fact the nude image she later produced looked the same in the front as it did in the behind view.

Maybe she didn't want to shock the nuns by producing real-life explicit areas. Also familiar was a girl from Mexico who spoke English with a heavy Spanish inflection. Her high cheek bones, slightly tilted deep-set black eyes, coal-black hair, and full mouth proclaimed her Indian and Spanish ancestry. She was stunning and exotic.

The next girl to enter the room was tiny, so quick and light on her feet that I was sure she was a refugee from some grade school who had wandered into the wrong place. She was Alice Hurford, only fifteen, a brilliant art student who was to be a freshman at Maryville in the fall.

"Are we all here?" asked Schlitvisky, turning around to face the group after adjusting his smock to the best advantage.

"Just a minute! Just a minute!" The sound came from outside the room and burst on our ears as a bundle of excitement and perpetual motion stumbled through the doorway. The last member of the class had arrived. Her name was Marie Catlin. Mother Mouton had told me about her on the phone.

She had won a scholarship to a technical school, which emphasized the arts.

She had done so well there that she had been taking courses all over the city paid for by her school. She was not what you could call a pretty girl, but willing to please, and ravenous for knowledge. Later she was to become internationally known in her chosen field with her work in major museums throughout the world.

In the days and weeks that followed, Alice and I became fast friends. We had the same taste in books and laughed at the same kind of jokes. The professor told us it was necessary to build a clay model from the bones out, so he taught us anatomy first. He made sure we knew what we were about before we could put hands into the delicious looking, cool, mushy clay.

Finally one day Professor Schlitvisky told us we were ready to begin. He stood back and threw or rather slung his clay at an armature to show us how to start the form. Unfortunately, Marie had bent over in her eager way to pick up some clay, which had dropped on the floor as a result of Schlitvisky's zeal.

The next handful of clay landed squarely on that portion of Marie's anatomy that was most in evidence as she was leaning down on all fours.

"What the heck!" she screamed in her native tongue (Italian), blushing a deep crimson. The two nuns also blushed. And Ivan (as we called him from that point on) had the good manners to blush, himself. Alice and I didn't blush—we giggled. Ivan apologized to Marie, and the class returned to some semblance of order.

Ivan continually addressed the group as "children" in spite of the fact that at least one of the nuns was old enough to be his mother. Mother Crump and Mother Watkins always referred to him as Professor *Shit*visky whether in chaste innocence or with "malice aforethought" I never knew.

As our work progressed and a human body assumed shape on each individual armature, Ivan cajoled, complimented, or bullied each of us into doing her best work. He accompanied his suggestions with a constant chatter, making jokes at his own expense and laughing hilariously at any snide remark Alice or I might fling his way, especially if he thought such remarks apt in his case.

"Ah, those little sweet spots!" he would murmur to himself as his hand rounded a curve on one of the clay nudes, thoroughly embarrassing us all.

When Mother Mouton had said the class would be only in the mornings because of the heat, I could now appreciate what she meant. Universal air conditioning as we have it now was nonexistent, and if it hadn't been for the thick walls of the ancient building and the lofty ceilings, we would have been even more uncomfortable.

The afternoons in the near hundred-degree heat of the library were spent with perspiration slowly and endlessly trickling off Alice and me as we poured over book after book, checking, binding pages, fitting and sealing new covers. All this to the accompanyment of the depressing war news. The situation in North Africa was becoming impossible, yet we continued to listen to the radio in the library every day as if by thus punishing ourselves we could share the agony of our Allies.

At the end of each day, I ached all over. I felt as if my whole body were sprained. My arms ached from working with the clay all morning. My neck had developed a permanent kink from bending over the books all afternoon.

The high point of the day was *gouter*, the French substitute for Tea. Sister Jennings, who was in charge of the kitchen at Maryville, prepared and served clandestine *gouter* to us in a small pantry off the main dining room. She always greeted us with kind words, "Sure and ye mud daubers need a bit of refreshment after strugglin' with thet mess o mud ye're stirrin' up in that room down there. Mind ye don't track up me clean floors with yer mud daubin. Sech goins on I niver saw the likes of! Nakid ladies of mud in this lovely school! The saints be praised and the Riverind Mither o the whole order is comin' soon to see what kind o mess ye're makin' and ye'll all be shamed o yirselves then. be gorra!"

When the Reverend Mother did put in her appearance, she was so shocked to see that we were actually making nude statues. During her entire visitation at the college, she religiously turned her head and averted her eyes whenever she came within the remotest vicinity of the rec room.

Moe had been having a rather gruesome time at her playground job. The children were tough and unmanageable. I met Moe every evening at the streetcar stop, which was halfway between Maryville and her playground. She usually looked as if she had been worked through a washing-machine wringer. Her beautiful slim body slumped in dejection many nights as she waited for me. I could tell she had had a particularly trying day by the frown between her tired eyes and the thin, grim look of her mouth. One day she won over the toughest boy, and after that, she had less trouble. She instructed while he kept the children in line. But it was very hard for her. I felt guilty because what I was doing was really much easier.

I enjoyed what I was doing and had made a good friend in Alice Hurford.

Every day Sister Jennings's extra snack energized me enough to drag myself to the streetcar stop. There Maureen and I boarded the first trolley of three, which would finally deposit us in Webster Groves. Maureen still sometimes wore a look of despair at this point. She had been coping with tough kids on the playground all day. One day they even threw her in the playground pool. I knew on that day, at least, that she was cooler than I was.

The first street car would usually be packed with people going home from work, but the crush would be heaviest on the Manchester Trolley, to which we transferred at the Old Courthouse. The pressure of all our sweating bodies in 95 to 105 degree heat was taken for granted. There were never any empty seats when Maureen and I reached the second trolley. We stood up with all the other passengers, shifting from side to side or forward and backward as the street car lurched around sharp corners and miraculously avoided cars and trucks. The clanging of the warning bell and the laughter and tired conversations of other passengers were cozy background music for me as I hung on to a slippery metal post with one hand and held *Mein Kampf* or an *Introductory Book to Japanese Characters* in the other hand. I thought these two books might help me to better understand the enemy. Other street car sufferers probably thought me a spy and occasionally it did cause them to keep a few inches distance.

My olfactory nerves would be assaulted sometimes by the stench from the St. Louis Stockyards. This horrific smell blasted through the open windows if the wind were blowing in the wrong direction. As we passed St. Louis U's magnificent church every day, I said a silent prayer there would be at least *one* vacant seat when we reached Maplewood to transfer to the Brentwood line. Then Maureen and I could take turns sitting on it. What bliss! Sometimes there were even *two* vacant seats as we approached Webster. Sometimes there would be a waft of fresh-flower-scented breeze as we hurtled along amid green lawns and overhanging elms through Richmond Heights and dear Webster.

Finally we stumbled from the trolley at Holy Redeemer Church after disengaging ourselves from the hot seats. Usually our skirts would be stuck there and would make a ripping sound as we stood up and exited the car. Then we dragged ourselves down the long block of Joy Street and turned left at Hawthorne. The Chateau at Chenenceau in France never looked as beautiful to me as our old Victorian house did as Maureen and I gained the front steps. (The house had been built by the Avery family during the turn of the century. Our family rented it while my father served as U.S. District Attorney during the Roosevelt years. I had always wanted to live in a "Victorian Mansion" and didn't realized I *had* lived in one till many years later.)

At this point Maureen and I usually kicked off our shoes and grabbed a cold Coke from the fridge. We rested for a few minutes, sipping our soda pop because we knew we had to gain strength for what was ahead of us. Our mother's helpers had left her to take war jobs in the factories. Mother was having difficulty luring a cook and nursemaid to our home where eight children ran rampant. Neither Mother nor Maureen or I knew how to cook, but we soon learned. Mother mostly gave orders while we did the actual cooking. We called her "Queen of the Kitchen."

We had to set the table, cook dinner, wash and dry the dishes, then bathe the two youngest little boys and tuck them into bed. And hope we could intercept the little fellows before they attacked our dates, who were usually servicemen and sometimes would also be invited for dinner. You see, our two youngest brothers had the annoying habit of jumping from the stairway landing and hanging onto the surprized young men's necks until they would pay the little boys nickels or dimes to disengage. One young man refused to pay tribute and was rewarded with a cold slimy fish slipped into his pocket.

In addition to local talent, who were usually in the reserves at Washington U. or St. Louis U., servicemen we had known years before as kids at the beach in Michigan or brothers or cousins of friends or friends of friends or even sons of my mother's college friends of World War I vintage were usually camping at our house at dinnertime.

They were being processed at Jefferson Barracks or Lambert Field or passing through St. Louis on their way to other airfields or naval bases. Sometimes we recruited these guests to help with the dishes, which Maureen and I washed, wearing our bathing suits if the evening were especially humid and torrid. The sister who washed the dishes had the privilege of throwing the dirty dishwater at the other who had merely dried. Then we took turns mopping the floor with the spilled dishwater, as Mother liked to have her kitchen floor mopped every day.

My sister and I were also initiated into washing the family clothes. We hooked up an extension line from the kitchen to the old-fashioned roller-type washing machine, which we had moved to the back yard. We thought this was fun because this duty was also performed in our bathing suits. After the clothes were washed and wrung out, we threw the last rinse water at each other to cool off.

For our official War Duties, in addition to cooking for visiting soldiers, sailors, marines, airmen, and one refugee from the British "Black Watch," we joined the Girls Service Organization, which regularly gave dances and parties at Lambert Field for the Free French and Royal Air Force cadets from the British Isles. The G.S.O. also gave private parties at larger homes in Webster for American servicemen.

Since my father was the Federal D.A. during our high school and college years, sometimes this led to some embarrassing situations for all concerned. At one point in our dating careers, Moe was dating the son of the most notorious bookie in that part of the mid-South at the same time I was dating the son of a man my father was currently trying a case against in Federal court. This boy's father ended up in federal prison, but my father never did connect the fellow his daughter was dating with the man he had to send to prison. Another young man I had a terrible crush on was the son of an attorney whom my father had just vanquished in an important trial. One night after a date, Ed and I were standing on the front porch from which we could see through the glass panels of the door. We watched my father sneak down the back stairs in his underwear and then raid the fridge.

"There goes the opposition in his B.V.D.s" gasped my date. "I wish my father could see this show!"

Sometimes a strange young man would show up at the door and announce that Cousin Grace or Aunt Kitty had told him to look up the Blantons. We were always glad to have one, two, or three extra in addition to our own seven siblings for dinner.

Mother, who was nearsighted, sat at one end of the table. Taking advantage of this situation, Moe and I would sometimes set the place of some unsuspecting sailor, fly-boy, or marine, with a butcher knife, spatula, and egg-beater instead of the usual knife, fork, and spoon. Usually the victim would be too flabbergasted or well mannered to complain. He would sit stoically with watering mouth until one of us took pity on him and exchanged his weapons for more conventional tools.

One night when I was particularly exhausted from my mud-daubing and household duties, a young man, who said Aunt Kitty sent him, knocked at our front door. He said to me, "Little girl, is your mother home?"

I had been playing baseball with my little brother Harry and was barefooted, in shorts, and floppy shirt, my hair in pigtails, and my speechless mouth had no lipstick. What a predicament! No wonder he thought I was a little girl.

I took one good look at this character and thought, "WOW!!! What a hunk of a man." I scurried upstairs, told Mother she had a visitor, and transformed my appearance in five minutes flat.

My hair came down, my feet went up (propped in my newest platform shoes). I put on my prettiest dress, a blue Persian print that did all the right things for my ninety-pound shape. I dashed down the stairs like a mild hurricane before one of my sisters could see this man and put the snatch on him.

The tall, handsome soldier waited patiently at the foot of the stairs as I came down. He looked at me with eyes so brilliantly green that they seemed to shimmer and glow with an inner light. You might call them neon-eyes.

"Where did you come from?" he asked when I had run through the reception hall again.

"I'm the little girl who just let you in the door a few minutes ago. Who are you, anyway?" I asked, trying not to appear too eager.

"I'm Tom Kavanagh. Your Grandma is my Aunt Kittie's best friend up in Bay City, Michigan. She's been begging me for months to come out here and meet you and your charming sisters. I'm stationed at the Air Base. Aunt Kitty said she especially wanted me to meet Rosemary. Are you Rosemary?

I'm sure my face must have fallen at least a foot. I was so dismayed. My sister Rosemary was two years older, very beautiful, and sophisticated *and* practically engaged to two men at the same time. I was sure she didn't need this stunning Greek God and I certainly did.

"Oh, Rosemary isn't your type," I began.

"How do you know that?"

"Because she's just the opposite of me, and I *am* your type."

Tom chuckled in appreciation. Rosemary was very delightful and was quite put out with Moe and me at college proms and fraternity dances because we would jitterbug and display our prowess with other dance fads, too. Rosemary considered dancing jitterbug "vulgar and common." Sometimes she pretended she didn't even know us if she considered our conduct particularly rambunctious. I can't say I blamed her, for one night I was dancing at a U.S.O. dance with such patriotic fervor that the entire left side of my formal split open on the dance floor. I had to spend the rest of the dance in the powder room. I came out only when I was sure the party was over and all the servicemen safely removed from the scene.

All of this stuff flashed through my mind as I stared at this perfect man! He was absolutely God's gift to women. I didn't want to appear immature.

The rest of that first evening, I divided my time between staring at his marvelous chiseled features and listening to his deep rich voice. It seemed to envelope me in a spell, its warm booming syllables permeating my entire being, heating up my bloodstream, tickling my pituitary gland, causing my adrenalin to shoot around with wild abandon in a counterclockwise motion. Every witticism he made, every smile he gave me, made butterflies in regular colonies raise general bedlam in my innards. He must have noticed me, too, as I received the following note in the mail two days later.

> Pat,
>
> Often in pursuit of the military, one forgets that delight is still existent until one meets again that lilting, wholesome philosophy such as yours and things don't seem so bad after all. Unless it be as the poet says,
>
> Ah, that Spring should vanish with the rose,
> And life's sweet-scented manuscript should close,
> The bird that in the willow sang, is gone
> But alas, where? Who knows?"
>
> Omar Khayyam
>
> Seriously, Pat, I did enjoy being with you and your family last night and hope it won't be long until I have the privilege of seeing you again,
>
> Tom Kavanagh

Now you can see from that epistle that he was overly cautious not to use one word of endearment, even the routinely accepted "dear" in the salutation and "yours" or some substitute in the closing. I knew he must have felt something or he wouldn't have been so hell-bent to avoid even the most unassuming of affectionate terms. To borrow a phrase from Will Shakespeare, "Me thought he did protest too much."

Also there was definitely a hint from this reader of poetry that he would like to be invited to our house again.

I replied with a quotation of my own:

> Tom,
> All right, I suppose that means you want to come out again.
> You might as well come for dinner Sunday, because,
> "It is hard for an empty sack to stand upright."
> —Ben Franklin
>
> As ever?
> Pat

Tom came for dinner the next Sunday. In addition to looking handsome, this time he also looked mysterious. He was wearing a pair of sunglasses although it had been raining hard all day.

Tom had been made a sergeant during the week and, unfortunately for him, he had met up with a private gone psycho who didn't appreciate sergeants. This character had screamed out, "I hate non-coms!"

He had punched the unprepared and very new Sergeant Tom Kavanagh very hard on one of his gorgeous green eyes. His left green eye was now also black and blue. I thought this just made him look more interesting.

As he explained the intricacies of playing chess to me and admired my paintings, which I proudly showed him, I realized this was the man I had been waiting for all twenty years of my life. He came out to our house unannounced several more times that summer to find that I was out almost every time, usually at parties for U.S. servicemen or for European cadets. The last time he just appeared at our door, expecting me to be there waiting for him, I suppose.

I was at a dance in honor of R.A.F. cadets who were in training at Lambert Field. These boys were mostly from England and Scotland, although some few were from New

Zealand and Australia. One fair Britisher, a graduate of Oxford, told me he didn't care to mingle with the common people when I asked him to dance during a "Ladies' Choice" set of dances. I had noticed him standing by himself all evening, and I was just trying to be kind.

This fellow said to me, "I will not be able to dance with you because I would have to get too close to the crowd of commoners on the dance floor."

Naturally, I left him to brood in solitary glory as he unmingled all by himself for the rest of the evening. I danced away with a darling Scotsman who came out for dinner the following Sunday.

At that same dance, Moe met a charming boy from London, who called her the next day. She told me later about their phone conversation.

"I say, are you there?"

"Who is this?"

"Oh, well, it's Jeffrey, you know, one of the chaps from the R.A.F. I say, I'm free tonight and hopping about—are you interested?"

Moe replied, "I'm sorry but I can't understand you very well. You sound as if you're speaking with something in your mouth."

"I have my pipe in my mouth."

"Would you mind taking it out so I can understand what you're saying?"

"Do I have to? Oh, then, all right. Will you go out with me tonight?"

"I'd love to. What time?"

"Sevenish."

"Okay."

"Smashing!"

Now Tom Kavanagh would never have done anything as easy and ordinary as phoning me for a date ahead of time. He would just appear occasionally at our front door unannounced. When he *did* catch me home, he was very careful never to say anything the least bit entangling. The more I liked him, the scarcer he got.

We had finished our full-length nude clay figures at the sculpturing class and had almost completed our head, neck, and shoulders of a female, which are called "busts." My younger brothers couldn't understand why the second statue was called a bust when that interesting part was *not* included. Several members of the class were fortunate enough to have their figures cast in bronze, but I didn't have the nerve to ask my parents for that favor. When Mother and Daddy came to view the work I had slaved over for months, Daddy said, "Very nice, Patricia, very nice."

Mother said, "Well, I suppose it's interesting."

After those remarks I justly felt my poor statues had been "Damned with faint praise." But the bust the genius Marie had modeled in clay was going to be cast in bronze and placed in a position of honor at her school. And it seemed to my disappointed ego that Marie had unconsiously used me for her model. Her statue had the same shape as my head, the same long hair, deep-set eyes, high cheekbones, cleft in the chin. And that was definitely my nose—kind of long with a bump, but ending in an acceptable Irish tilt at the end.

When Grandma Daily, Aunt Kittie's best friend in Bay City, realized that I had worked hard all summer on clay models without having them cast, she made a special trip to Detroit. She was a very talented painter, herself, and knew how unfulfilled I must have been. Grandma made a grand tour of Detroit's best art galleries. She found what she was looking for—a painting, which she thought would make up for my disappointment. She bought the painting for me and lugged it all the way down to St. Louis on the Wabash Cannonball.

This oil painting was a nude but could not have aroused even the Mother Superior at school. It showed the back, upper shoulders, and head of a lady in her bath and looked quite a bit like I did in a similar condition. Grandma called it, "Patricia's Modest Nude."

I saw Tom for the last time the day he was transferred to a base in North Carolina. He finally called me the night before but only to tell me he was leaving by train from Union Station the next day, but due to packing, etc., would *not* be able to come out to the house to tell me good-bye personally.

The next day was Saturday, and Alice Hurford and I decided to go down to Union Station to say good-bye to Tom. There were two trains leaving for North Carolina, and I was there in time to see both of them pull out of the station.

The station was so crowded with servicemen that it was almost impossible to find a particular face in that mass of people and uniforms. Five minutes before the time of departure of the last train, I recognized Tom from a distance. He saw me at the same moment and rushed over to where I was standing. He took my hand, which was cold and clammy in spite of the fact that the temperature was hanging around the hundred degree mark. A flow of electricity surged up my arm, causing my face to blush after taking a detour to my heart, which began to pound dangerously.

"Good-bye, Pat—it's been wonderful knowing you," he said.

The one person I really wanted in the world was saying good-bye! I knew I would never see him again.

That last tragic sentence would have been considered a happy ending by dear Tom, probably, if he had known what was in store for him. Two months later as my friend Angie and I were on the Wabash Cannonball heading for a football weekend in Detroit, Tom walked into our car and I knew it was fate—we would surely see each other again.

Two years later between air raids, flights to North Africa, etc., and while I was engaged to marry several other characters, Tom began to write to me, then suddenly appeared in St. Louis and courted me strenuously. The first time he asked me to marry him, of course I said yes. It had taken him over two years to get around to asking me the first time, and I knew if I turned him down just to play hard to get it might be another five years or *never* before he asked me again.

It was January of 1945. I was engaged to marry Tom, my handsome Greek God Air Force Lieutenant, but my wedding preparations had become a nightmare. My mother insisted on having everything done exactly according to Emily Post. I thought it more according to the N.C.A.A. rules because by the time the fatal day approached, the tug of war between my mother and myself had become an athletic contest.

My darling long-suffering mother who had nursed me through various commonplace childhood diseases and a few exotic ones, such as malaria fever, my mother who had put up with my quirks and whimsies through the years I had dabbled in painting, sculpting, acting, modeling, and now writing, my good friend and champion who had even made a novena for me to marry the proper man and who had her prayers answered by my handsome airman's sudden appearance on the last day of the novena—this darling woman was now locked in mortal combat with me over wedding plans.

She thought it would be lovely if I wore my sister Rosemary's wedding dress, which was beautiful and "could be taken in at the seams and up at the hem to fit me with no trouble at all." I objected. I was the second oldest daughter and had worn hand-me-downs many times before, but I absolutely refused to wear my sister's hand-me-down wedding gown.

Mother said, "If you want a long white wedding gown of your own, you'll have to pay for it yourself." So I added that item to the rest of the trousseau I was buying with my meager salary. I was copywriter and editor of the "House Organ" of one of the big downtown St. Louis stores. Using the store as a base, I toured the shops and argued with my mother over everything. We looked at veils and more veils but couldn't agree on type or price. Finally she said, "If you want such a long veil, you'll have to use one of your wedding checks for it. I'm not going to pay for it." So Great-aunt Lizzie's check went for the veil.

It was a perfectly lovely creation, topped by a juliet cap made of delicate old lace from my mother's wedding gown. (My younger sister Maureen was happy to wear it two years later with no remarks about having to wear a hand-me-down.) Then there was the matter of china. Mother thought it would be practical if I chose the same Lennox pattern she had. Then she could leave her set to me some day to enlarge mine. I refused this offer. I wanted to pick my own pattern.

Mother thought an all-military wedding would be beautiful. She wanted the groom, the best man, and the ushers all in Air-Force dress white. The only obstacle here was that none of the men in the wedding party could or would put out the money for such a grand show. And Tom had asked his older brother, a civilian, to be best man.

The number and identity of the bridesmaids were other bones of contention. My mother was the only daughter in a prominent and well-to-do Michigan family. *Her* mother had seen that she attend a prestigious women's college on the East Coast. She attended parties at the White House in designer gowns. She studied opera in New York and sang the part of Juliet in a college production of *Romeo & Juliet.* She was "Belle of the Ball." at Annapolis "hops." Now it was her turn to pass on her status quo to her daughters. She wanted me to choose my bridesmaids from some of my more aristocratic and socially prominent friends.

Mother said, "That will make the write-ups in the newspapers more interesting." This plan was all right with me, but I also insisted on having my good friend who lived next door, the groom's sister, and my two younger sisters for bridesmaids. The size of the bridal party would alternately expand and contract according to the mood Mother and I were in on any given day.

I was the happiest bride in all Missouri when the formal wedding in St. Louis was canceled because Tom's leave was canceled. He had received his orders to go overseas immediately. We were married at his port of embarkation. I wore my long white satin gown and the Aunt Lizzie veil, though I had to carry them all the way to Fort Myers, Florida, on several trains and busses.

My mother went along as chaperone. With all the fussy wedding plans now a thing of the past, we were good friends and companions again. Our trip to Fort Myers became very complicated, though. There had been a terrible accident several miles south of us, and our engine had gone back up north after switching our Pullman car and the dining car off the main line. We were left on an unused siding someplace between Jacksonville and Tampa supposedly to stay there only until the tracks were cleared. However, someone must have forgotten us. We sat and fumed on that siding for over twenty-four hours.

When an engine was finally sent to take us on to Tampa, six sailors, who had been celebrating something or other the entire time and sleeping in only two upper berths in alternating shifts, decided it would be fun to pull the emergency cord to stop the train every twenty minutes or so.

Meanwhile the frantic bridegroom waiting in Fort Myers thought he had been jilted. He called our home in St. Louis, looking for me. My father yelled into the phone, "She's someplace in the state of Florida!"

The wedding finally took place at the missionary church in Fort Myers. There were only six people in the church. They were the groom, the bride, the best man (an unknown captain recruited by Tom from the Officers' Club the night before), my mother, who was my one and only attendant as fate would have it, and a sweet old nun who cried all the way through the ceremony as she gallantly played the organ, and of course the officiating priest, Father O'Reardon. Tom walked down the aisle with me before and after the ceremony. I guess he gave me away to himself. He took the place of my father before the ceremony. Daddy was too busy bringing enemy aliens to justice. He was the wartime U.S. Attorney in St. Louis and couldn't be spared. He couldn't waste two or three days chasing around the country trying to get to my wedding.

I had insisted on a double-ring ceremony. We had practiced the whole scheme for the wedding the night before. When Father O'Reardon learned that Tom had attended Notre Dame and had actually played football there, he devised a sort of T-square formation for the exchange of wedding rings. Tom practiced placing his ring on my finger, and then he moved in a square to the left around me as I moved in a square to the right of him. Then I placed my ring on his finger.

On the morning of the wedding, however, Tom got tangled in the long train of my wedding dress. We had one terrible time getting untangled. Father O'Reardon stopped dead in the midst of the ceremony and glared at me.

"Pat," he yelled in his Irish brogue, "Why didn't ye tell me ye were goin' to wear a train five miles long?" And to the stronger looking of the two altar boys, he said, "You—Jimmy, never mind servin' the Mass. It's your job from now on to take care of Pat's train!"

At the end of the Wedding Mass, my satin dress was still presentable. My mother treated our tiny wedding party to a grand brunch at a local restaurant. Tom and I walked a few blocks to the site, and the rest of the party taxied over. My mother and I were great friends, and I was Tom's bride.

The Blanton family in St. Louis in 1945.

Recipe with a History

When I was a young lady, fried chicken was the main course in just about everyone's favorite summer Sunday dinner south of the Mason-Dixon line.

As World War II was drawing to a close, my husband, an Air Force Combat Intelligence Officer, was still stationed in the European Theatre; my sister Rosemary's husband, an officer with the Signal Corps, was still in the Pacific War Zone. He would be privileged soon to be on the *Missouri* during the signing of the peace treaty with Japan.

Our parents had graciously invited Rosemary and two babies and me to become a part of the household again until our husbands were shipped home. Mother and her children had moved back to southeast Missouri after my father's tenure as Federal District Attorney for the eastern half of Missouri was about over. President Truman had taken charge after President Roosevelt's death.

On a weekend pass, my brother John, appealing in his naval seaman's uniform, had brought a naval buddy with him for Sunday dinner. During our stay in St. Louis, renters at our Sikeston home had allowed the evergreens and other trees, shrubs and flowers, to grow unchecked and untrimmed. My father's five acres at the edge of our small town had become a wildlife sanctuary for thousands of starlings and smaller birds from Missouri, Illinois, Kentucky, Tennessee, and Arkansas. Their comings and goings morning and evening sounded like an invading foreign airforce from Europe and the Pacific.

My mother had arranged for some construction work done to the old house before our move back South. Our cook, Ruby, who had moved to St. Louis years before when we did, had now agreed to move back temporarily to the country with us.

She was enthroned in her place in the kitchen on this particular Sunday, but her usual prompt dinner had not appeared on the dining-room table yet. My mother, my father—who was down for the weekend—and extended family were becoming hungry and restless.

"Patricia, Ruby and you always have been good friends. Will you please go out to the kitchen and see what's holding up dinner? I'm sure she won't resent your help if she needs it," my mother pleaded.

I pushed through the swinging door from the dining room to the pantry and on to the kitchen.

Ruby was bent double, her whole body shaking. I rushed over to her and put an encouraging arm around her. "What's the matter, Ruby? Why are you crying?" I asked.

"I'm not crying, I'm laughing," she said. "This gravy won't pour. It just bounces."

"Where did you get the flour to thicken it?" I asked.

"Why, up here in the flour bin, where it's always kept," Ruby replied.

I reached my hand up inside the bin and pulled out a paper bag, which announced in large letters, "WALLPAPER PASTE."

"Oh, Lordie, Lordie," Ruby gasped, "I used that stuff to fry the chicken with too!"

I dashed to the phone after informing Mother of the situation. The decorator yelled through the phone, "It's not lethal. Eat your dinner in peace. That's one meal that will stick to everybody's ribs, Miss Patricia."

The family and weekend guests finally gathered around the dining-room table. Mother passed out the different dishes, shaking as she did so. When she laughs too hard, she cries.

"This is the best fried chicken I've ever had," said John's guest. Everyone tore into the dinner and finished off the chicken in record time. Everyone except Mother and me. Here's the recipe for our family's southern fried chicken with adjustments for present interest in heart-safe cooking.

Recipes

Old-Time Recipe
(World War Vintage)

—half a pound of lard
—one large chicken—cut up
—enriched flour in big brown bag (preferably not PASTE)
—salt and pepper
—one large skillet (iron)

Turn fire under iron skillet with lard (on high).

Shake pieces of chicken in brown bag after salting and peppering same.

Place chicken in skillet.

Place top on skillet.

When chicken becomes brown and crispy, turn over with fork, turn down heat to very slow, and place top back on skillet. Shake more salt, pepper, and parsley on chicken. Cook for about 30 minutes.

New Life-Saving Recipe

—enough olive oil to cover bottom of skillet (iron)
—a large Amish-raised chicken (skinned and cut up)
—Mrs. Dash's spices
—garlic powder
—Italian seasoning
—parsley flakes

Turn fire under skillet on high.

Shake chicken pieces in brown bag with unbleached flour and seasonings.

Place chicken in hot olive oil.

Place top on skillet.

Turn over when chicken is brown and crispy.

Place top back on skillet and cook about 30 minutes on low heat, shaking more seasoning on pieces.

Amid War Shortages, Abundance, the Fort Shelby Caper

In the olden days, when I was in college, nice girls lived in dorms. If *still* not married after graduation, they continued to live under the parental roof until married however long that might take.

I know only one girl whose parents allowed her to live that exciting apartment life while still in school. And that was because she and a younger sister shared the apartment with a fastidious older sister whose eagle eye supervised their activities.

So, until my Air Force husband returned from overseas duty in 1946, I, who had always wanted to live in an apartment, had never actually done so. We had been married only a few weeks before he was sent with his squadron to a base in England. We had lived in hotel rooms or a small rented room in someone else's home during the very short time we were together in the States.

When he returned from Europe in 1946, I was so excited about the prospect of finally becoming an apartment-dweller in a big city. But apartments were impossible to find. We looked and looked. We scanned the "For Rent" ads in both big city newspapers hungrily. We finally settled for a room at the Fort Shelby Hotel. It would give us a few weeks to really go apartment hunting on Saturdays. For a month we looked at apartments every spare moment. Two of them I will never forget.

The first apartment we looked at was a puzzlement, at least to me who had led an overprotected life. There were at least fifteen phones in the small messy flat. I couldn't figure it out—who would need fifteen phones? Although there would be a line for each of Tom's five siblings and my own seven siblings not to mention concerned parents. In case of an emergency, they could all call at the same time.

Tom burst out laughing when he saw the setup. "This must have been a bookie joint before it was raided. No way would I consider this place!" he bellowed.

The other apartment building that remains in my memory was really revolting. Trash and garbage lined the halls, and the overpowering odor of cabbage and garlic blasted from each open transom and door and snaked its way out under those that were shut. My olfactory nerves were assaulted, and my queasy stomach was doing flip-flops that would make any Olympic gymnast look like a piker.

Inside the advertised apartment, many giant roaches sashayed about the living room, bedroom, and of course, the kitchen. They seemed to be enjoying themselves dancing, darting here and there in pairs, in chorus lines, sometimes pausing in their frenzied activity to confer with one another. Ugh!

After several more weekends of similar excursions, Tom and I were ready to give up and continue living in our two-dollar a day room at the Fort Shelby. Finally, through one of my husband's uncles, we heard of a vacant apartment to rent in the Clark Park Apartments. We went to look at this vacant number and could hardly believe what we found.

What bliss! What joy! No roaches! Clean, freshly painted walls. It was a tiny studio apartment with a charming bed that would be pulled out of the wall. Then Tom would slam it back into the wall before he left for work in the morning. I only hoped I would be awake and out of the bed before he did the slamming.

There was also a studio couch, which would accommodate any possible visitor from either side of the family. All of this in the large, airy living room. No matter that the air was laden with dust and soot from the city I so desperately longed to live in. The view from the two large living room windows was a view of two similar large living room windows in the neighboring apartment building two feet away. No sunshine ever entered our precious apartment—but who cared? It was clean, freshly painted, bugless, cozy, and it was ours.

In the tiny kitchen was a miniature stove. There was also a mini fridge. A table and two chairs painted Chinese Red graced the far end of the kitchenette. The color came on like a Chinese dragon, but at least it woke me up every morning. I couldn't even look in the direction where I knew the coffee pot was to be hidden for the next few months. The very thought of the rich potent aroma of coffee would send me running to the immaculate bathroom.

I suffered morning sickness every morning for four months. Only my nausea lasted all day and night. I was expecting our first baby, about to live in a building in which the manager had told us "no pregnancies or babies allowed."

Luckily for us Clark Park was at our door as well as a small park at the end of West Grand Boulevard, facing the Detroit River. We could sit there, and dream of the future, and watch the freighters go by. We took the apartment without further ado.

We had a very tight budget due to the meager take-home pay of $218 a month the I.R.S. provided us with. We had Government bonds stashed away and were buying another one each month in hopes of buying a little bungalow soon. It was a challenge to work out a shopping list and menus that wouldn't gag us on the ten dollars a week we decided we could spare for food.

We shopped once a week. We used the fresh meat (hot dogs and hamburger) toward the beginning of the week and canned meals such as spaghetti and tuna fish for Thursday and Friday. There was always an emergency can of beans and miniature weenies for nights when we miscalculated or unexpected company appeared. This special can cost ten cents. I also saved pop bottles and grease to sell to the supermarkets. I felt no compunction about picking up abandoned bottles from vacant lots. This extra income was used for special emergencies, such as a visit from a Bay City grandma or a St. Louis brother or sister. Otherwise these visitors would have placed too heavy a burden on our fragile budget.

Along with balancing our budget, we had another problem with shortages. The toilet-tissue shortage wasn't so easy to solve. The stuff had become so precious it was almost contraband—definitely for under-the-counter customers. We, as newcomers, were extended no special courtesies by the neighborhood shop-keepers, and we were desperate.

I decided that, as long as the emergency existed, I would combine our need to do something about it with the opportunity to have a Saturday night date with my husband.

We looked forward all week to our date. I would put on my most presentable dress, a bargain holdover from my sparse wartime trousseau of the year before. Luckily for my expanding waist, there was an insert of elastic at the back. I saved my one pair of high heels for this important weekly event because I could not afford to have the heels repaired if they should wear down.

My purse was a big bag because storage space was a must. I'd also wear a jacket with large pockets.

Tom and I would catch the bus for downtown, eat a Coney Island hot dog, and then stop off at the Fort Shelby. Living there those two months made us feel the dear old establishment was our home. We also felt that it owed us something for our patronage.

It was thus that we would "borrow" handfuls of toilet tissue from the hotel's generously supplied rest rooms. I would stuff it into my whopper purse and all the pockets of my jacket. Tom would emerge from the men's room with a poker face and bulging pockets. We hoped each foray would supply us through the week.

We spent the rest of our date looking at the *Free Press* Sunday funnies in the lobby or watching other people fish at the edge of the Detroit River. We couldn't afford a fishing pole, but we were happy. Our ten-dollar food allotment had seen us through another week safely, we had each other, and the longed-for baby was on its way. That wonderful apartment was waiting for us at the end of the date. Who could ask for anything more?

Grandma's Love Affair with the Statler

If my grandma were alive today, I'm sure she'd manage a way to save the Statler Hotel. Detroit's Statler was her very favorite hotel in the whole world. It would have broken her heart to see her beloved Statler, her home away from home, called by the unfamiliar name, "The Heritage," without electricity, rooms unoccupied, out of business! She wouldn't have believed it possible.

Grandma loved to travel and always stayed at the Statler if there happened to be one in the city she was visiting. Detroit's Statler was tops on her list because there was usually someone on the staff from Bay City she could persuade to give her V.I.P. treatment. Or someone who especially appealed to her who, she thought, might need managing or mothering.

Grandma was always managing to help or save some person or cause. From the time she was a child, she was controlling situations, usually to help someone save face.

One day when she was reminiscing about her childhood, she told me about one of her uncles:

> My Uncle Malcolm was a great burly fellow, about six feet three. He played the bagpipes. He had come over from the Scottish Hebrides with my mother. He was always bragging about how strong he was.
>
> One night at a party we were having at our house, he insisted he was so strong he could crack a walnut with his bare hand. Someone called his bluff and handed him a walnut. He strained and strained, but it wouldn't crack even a wee bit. He

> was getting all red in the face. If he couldn't crack that nut, he'd never be able to face his family and friends again.
>
> I sized up the situation. I sneaked out to the kitchen and cracked a walnut with a metal nutcracker. I crept back, unnoticed into the parlor.
>
> I slipped the broken nut into Uncle Malcolm's empty hand. Uncle Malcolm put both hands behind his back, exchanged the nuts, and then presented his open hand with the cracked walnut to the astonished crowd. I had saved the day for him!

Yes, she had saved the day for him. She continued to do it for various friends in various situations for the rest of her life. When she was a young married woman with two small children, her husband's mercantile business failed. A brother-in-law, a very successful businessman, then considered asking my grandpa to become a partner in a new wholesale grocery business. But this man had difficulty deciding between my grandfather and another successful businessman in their town, Bay City.

My grandma heard "by the grapevine" that the brother-in-law was going to seek the advice of a mutual friend before he made his final decision. My grandma got to the friend (a former beau) first and persuaded him to recommend my grandfather for the position. He followed her suggestion, and Grandpa Daily was the new partner in Tanner & Daily, securely established in a very elegant building. It was formerly the Opera House, host to many a celebrity during the booming lumbering days.

By arranging for her husband's getting the position in the new partnership, unknown to him, she not only saved Grandpa D's pride but brought security to her family for generations to come.

When she was middle-aged and her children had left home and her husband was doing well and no one in the family was within the range of her managing, she managed the lives of friends and neighbors.

A friend of hers who was much younger was in love with a man who was of a different religion. The girl's father forbade her to marry her suitor because of this religious difference.

Grandma heard gossip that the young lady was defying her father. She was planning to elope and go to a justice of the peace to marry her young man. When Grandma heard this bit of news, her comment was, "That will never do. I'll have to arrange something!" And as usual, she did.

Grandma arranged for them to be married privately by a clergyman. The day before the wedding, she took the young lady shopping. Grandma bought a lovely complete trousseau for the bride-to-be and charged the whole thing to the disapproving father's account at Wendland's store. Mr. Wendland was Grandma's good friend and neighbor.

When Grandma became exhausted from her busy life of managing her own, her family's, and her friends' lives, she traveled around the North American continent to relax, and if possible, to relax at the local Statler if there was one in that particular city.

When she reached her eighties, she was still arranging things for everyone, and still traveling and relaxing at the Statler, usually the one in Detroit. She now suffered from hardening of the arteries of the brain and the resultant loss of memory.

Because she often forgot where she was going or *why* she had gone to a certain place, if she did reach her destination, her son, my Uncle Lewie, persuaded her to stay with some longtime friends in their apartment when she announced, "I'd like to go down to Detroit for a visit!" Uncle Lewie thought she'd better have someone who was concerned keep an eye on her.

The day after Grandma arrived in Detroit for this, which would be her last visit, the lady she had come to visit phoned me to say, "Patricia, your Grandma has run away. I went out to the grocery store, and when I returned, she was gone. She left this note: 'I'm off to Battle Creek for a rest cure!' "

Grandma had been to Battle Creek for rest and relaxation several times many years before. I was panicked. I insisted to my husband, Tom, that we rush down to the railroad station to head her off and then bring her to our house until we could take her back to Bay City.

My husband reassured me, "Don't worry, honey. I know where your Grandma is. She's where she planned to be all along."

Tom dialed a number: The Statler and asked for Mrs. Daily's number. He was right! Her dear familiar voice answered the phone, "Hello, dears. What's the matter?"

Of course she had run away to her very favorite place, the Statler. Uncle Lewie brought her back to Bay City in a few days. Her traveling days would soon be over. A few weeks later, she fell and broke her hip. She was confined to a hospital bed at home for the rest of her life—only a few months. At least we knew where she was. There will never be another person like her.

The Baby Crow

Our ten-year-old son, Tommy, had an empathy for all animals, especially injured baby ones. In the park at the end of our block, he discovered a baby crow with a broken wing. Apparently it had been pushed or fallen out of the family nest. It seemed to have been abandoned by the mother bird.

Tommy brought the crow home and made a splint for the wing, with some instruction from his father. Our young son kept the baby bird in an abandoned rabbit hutch in the back yard. He fed it and nursed it back to health. He even gave it flying lessons.

The crow was soon restored in health and began making his presence felt and heard in the neighborhood and every morning at six A.M. would take on the role of neighborhood alarm clock. It cried out in a loud raspy voice not the usual crow call of, "Caw, Caw" but "MAW, MAW." After several days of this, the irate neighbor in the house behind us phoned us and asked to speak to my son. She said, "Tommy Kavanagh, tell your bird to SHUT UP!"

Our son replied, "He doesn't understand English. He just speaks crow talk."

"Well, then, let him go or I'll call the police!"

"Okay," my son said, tears running down his cheeks.

Tommy ran to the backyard and released the young crow. It immediately flew over our back yard fence and landed in the neighbor's tree where it continued to screech, "MAW, MAW!" This resulted in another phone call from the neighbor; "I thought I told you to let your bird go!"

Our son replied, "I did let that poor bird go. It's *your* bird now. It's in *your* tree. And by the way, tell your bird to be quiet. It's disturbing my sleep."

In a few minutes, dozens of small birds, sparrows and blue jays, attacked the young crow. I was afraid he would be killed. But the tender loving care he had received from Tommy came to his aid. With a strong burst of energy and a beautiful flight, he escaped his tormenters and headed for the park. There he was welcomed by a huge delegation of crows who surrounded and protected him.

Taxcut

The operation was going well, but the surgeon's assistant was emotionally involved with the patient. It took great self-control to avoid giving instructions to his superior.

The patient was our family pet—an English setter sporting the unlikely name of Taxcut. Luckily for the dog, the young veterinarian student had been home for the weekend when Taxi was run over by a car. The adventuresome puppy had climbed the backyard fence and set off to see what was on the other side of Six Mile Road.

He never found out. Not being sophisticated enough to cross with the green light, he had been hit by a car whose driver didn't bother to stop. Our son recognized the signs of shock. He and his father took Taxi to an emergency animal clinic in the neighborhood and then the next day to Michigan State University for the operation. His leg was broken, the bone shattered.

The operation was over at last. A pin had been inserted to hold the bones together. Soon Taxi was home again, handling his leg well. He lived thirteen more years and enjoyed an active and varied life.

His greatest joy was going "Up North" with my husband and me where he could run free in our forty acres at the "Tip o' the Mitt." He swam in our creek and raced down the trails. He "pointed" partridges and rabbits on the forty acres just as he had "pointed" honeybees and even flies on the forty-feet-wide back yard in Redford.

Going to and coming back from the northern property during necessary stops at McDonald's, Taxi always enjoyed a dessert of scraps from Big Macs after eating his regular dog food. On these trips he rode in his cage in the back of our old station wagon.

Two years ago a malignant tumor developed. Taxi had become completely blind. Arthritis added to his pain. Regretfully, the family decided it was time to end his misery. But on the way to the clinic, Taxi was allowed to ride on the front seat of the car, next to our son, now a Doctor of Veterinary Medicine. No more cage. And a stop was made at McDonald's where instead of scraps, he had a whole Big Mac of his own. He enjoyed it so much that "seconds" were ordered for him.

Concerning the First Day of Spring

Early this morning at about six-thirty, Annie said, "Hey, Mom, let's send in only two dollars with this cereal box top. We can get twenty kites!"

Of course we desperately needed twenty kites. Today is the first day of Spring.

It has been a very erratic winter. Whoever is in charge of these things has been playing games. On one night the temperature dropped forty degrees in one hour. We had

Rain
High winds
Then freezing rain
Sleet
Hail

And finally snow. All in one night. It has been like this all winter.

Now, at least, we seem to have a definite statement about the weather. Today is the first day of spring, and there is something about this day that lets you know it.

The snow is completely gone. Now we can see the lawns. They are still dull and depressing beige-brown. But the birds outside are singing, very excited about the days that are coming. The sun is shining in a business-like way. Its rays are spring rays, warm and caressing.

The children on their way home from school are shouting and laughing, calling out to one another as they skip and run.

The boy running fastest of all is Robbie. Last spring he was almost helpless. He had to lie in his red wagon while his sister and her friends took turns pulling him around the neighborhood. Both of his legs had been broken. His right leg was smashed when he was hit by a car and the left one, later on, when he fell down on the frozen creek in our park.

The trees are all straining to put out their buds. It's like a contest every year to see which trees will show green first. As usual, the staunch old weeping willows lining the creek have won the race. They are showing the slightest hint of green, and that is very faint and shy—a lovely pale chartreuse color, only a subtle whisper that spring has, indeed, returned today.

The melted snow has exposed the ugliness and untidiness of the backyards of all the prosaic look-alike houses in the neighborhood. Old toys and even a rusting lawn mower have been left out all winter in one yard. Maybe the people in that house had a great sadness last fall and didn't care about anything, especially their back yard. Maybe the soft spring days will comfort them and they will make a fresh start and plant flowers.

Our house is very quiet today. The usual loud inside the house winter noises are missing. There is no sound from the TV, record player or radio, no undercurrent of childish voices. The screams that tell us what room Sean is in have stopped. He is too busy working outside today to bother teasing the little girls. He is raking the front yard and feeding the soggy, muddy lawn his Boy Scout fertilizer.

The only noise heard in the house is the sound of our parakeet acting like a lovesick fool. The spring sunshine has activated his hormones. He is caged in our dining-room window, the sunshine streaming in on him, filtered by the evergreens and roof overhang.

He has become a sex maniac, furiously kissing his own reflection in his tiny mirror at least a thousand times a minute. He stops occasionally to burst into an exuberant aria. The rhythmic staccato of his pecking against the mirror contrasts mightily with his singing. He is torn between kissing the bird in the mirror and passionately serenading the curious wild birds that have returned to the still, stark bare branches of our yard trees.

These sojourners intermittently fly up to the porch to gaze in at the bright little tame bird in the dining-room window. He is safe but they are free, wise with the experience of flight over strange cities and seas.

Now someone has left the front door open, and the cool air is rushing in. I can hear the petulant voice of a mother who lives two houses down screaming at her daughter because she accidentally dropped one of her brand new shoes into the creek. There is going to be even more screaming on the next block when a kid from over there gets home. Sean just ran in to tell me that this kid decided to swim home down the polluted creek. Because it is all of 50 degrees outside now. This young boy just happens to have his entire new Easter outfit on.

The first fight among the neighborhood children has broken out. Although our two youngest daughters always fight between themselves and against Sean in the wintertime on the sleighing hill and on the skating pond, they do usually play agreeably with the neighbor children. But today there has been kicking, hair-pulling, and biting with their best friend, Ellen, as both victim and aggressor.

I punished my two by telling them they would have to stay inside the house for a while. Moonie told me that Ellen's mother had "grounded" her. She wouldn't be able to leave her own yard for two weeks.

Being a tender-hearted and irrational mother, after twenty minutes, I told these little girls they could go outside and even gave them each the money necessary to buy ice cream cones from the shop around the corner.

Now, in a few minutes later, I see them walking toward the house again, sharing every other lick with Ellen, their recent enemy. Ellen is the kid who was supposed to be grounded in her own yard for two weeks. As Bridget reaches the front door, she says,

> Mom, I forgot to tell you my teacher sent our whole class down to the Principal's office because we were marching from the front door of the school to the school bus instead of just walking like we usually do. That dumb teacher thought we were protesting something. We weren't protesting—we were just happy!

And these two little girls are no longer tracking snow through the front door onto the clean white tile of the front vestibule. They are now tracking in *mud!*

Spring is here!

Why It Was Hard for My Father to Say "I Love You"

"Get down from my magnolia tree right now, young man, before you break a limb!" My seventy-year-old father was yelling at my seven-year-old son one summer day about fourteen years ago.

Now just what kind of limb was he worried about? A limb on the tree or one of Sean's arms or legs?

Any of the secretaries at his office would have said, "Why, Miss Patricia, of course your father was talkin' about your son, when he was worried about 'breakin' a limb'! Everybody knows Mister Harry's the kindest, the most charmin' man in town, even if he *is* seventy!"

Any of the many people he had prosecuted and sent to the federal penitentiary when he was U.S. District Attorney in St. Louis might have said, "Of course the old buzzard meant the tree's limbs—he wouldn't care if his own grandson *did* fall! He was so hard he wasn't even human!"

But I, knowing everything I do know about my father, at last, understand that he meant both Sean's limbs and the tree's limbs—he wouldn't want either one to be broken, or even bruised.

To those who knew him only slightly, or through his profession or one of the various organizations he belonged to, my father appeared overly dignified, aloof, stern, and even cold. But, of course, even though, as a child I had never heard him say, "I love you," to me or anyone else in the family, I knew he *did* love us all very deeply because of the way he took care of us. He couldn't express his affection in words in those days. He had a reserved, serious nature and had an unusual boyhood.

My father was a strict disciplinarian with himself and made the attempt to be with his children. When I was a little girl, the discipline usually consisted of only a stern reprimand. Sometimes it was necessary only to give me a long, hard condemning look to cause my tears to flow and extract the necessary apology from me, "I'm sorry, I'll never do that again."

I can remember only two times that he actually spanked me. The first time he spanked my younger sister Maureen and me for cutting off the arms and legs of our older sister Rosemary's rag doll and then burying it in a shoebox under a favorite weeping willow tree. Maureen and I had a grand funeral for the doll, but Rosemary didn't appreciate it.

The second spanking was for picking all the blossoms off his Japanese Iris. This was when I was about five. I don't know *why* I did it, but I picked all the perfect blooms from the plants and then threw them across the lawn. That night when he came home from his office and saw the evidence on the grass, he asked me and my two sisters, "Who ruined my iris?" They wouldn't tattle on me, and I had no intention of tattling on myself, but I did give him this story.

"Daddy," I said, "I didn't do it—but I know who did!"

"Well, then, who did it, Patricia?"

"Daddy, I saw a darling pony come through the front gate and walk out here to the iris bed. I saw him take his right hoof and knock off each flower. Then, when he saw what a naughty thing he did, he was ashamed of himself and began to cry. Then he wiped away the tears with the same naughty hoof that broke the flowers."

"Now, Patricia," Daddy said, "you know that's just a story you made up. Did you pick the flowers?"

I couldn't understand why he didn't believe what I told him, but finally I had to admit I was the culprit. He gave me only two whacks on the backside instead of the expected three because, as he said, "I enjoyed your story, Patricia."

When I was nine, my Beagle puppy, Roxy, was run over and killed by a car. He died instantly and I was inconsolable. I cried all weekend, and my parents were afraid I was making myself sick; I couldn't eat or sleep, I was so upset.

My father had a conference with my grandfather, who was editor of the town newspaper. He wrote an editorial about the dear departed puppy, asking his readers for a substitute dog. There were several offers, and that night my father came home from work with a tiny new puppy peeking out of his overcoat pocket.

My sister Maureen and I shared a bedroom next to the "sleeping porch" where Daddy slept. His snoring kept Mother awake, and the crying of whoever was the new baby kept him awake, so they had separate bedrooms. When we were very young, Maureen and I were always terrified of thunderstorms. Anytime a severe storm was in progress, after every flash of lightning and clap of thunder, one of us would say in a loud whisper, "Daddy, we're both thirsty. Could we both have a drink of water?"

He would always answer, "Of course, Honeybunch," and then patiently get out of bed several times during the storm to bring us our drinks of water and never reprimand us.

Sometimes he would say, "What you really mean is, 'Daddy, I'm afraid,' isn't that right?" Then he'd take us out to the sleeping porch with him till the storm was over.

Tornadoes, or cyclones, as they were called down in Missouri Bootheel where we lived, were a danger that we took for granted every spring. Once during a cyclone, our family was huddled down in the basement when my sister Rosemary started crying.

"Don't be afraid, honey," Daddy said, "You're safe down here."

"I'm not crying for myself," she said, "I'm crying for my bird. I forgot to bring my canary down here."

My father just sighed and turned toward the stairs. He ran up the stairs and returned with Rosemary's little canary as we watched the storm through the basement windows. We saw shingles from our roof, shutters and a barn roof swept high as the wind howled and rolled.

He took us on many trips, mostly through the South and East because he wanted us to learn the history of our country, firsthand. We toured the battlefields of the "War between the States" and the Revolutionary War. He especially loved Virginia. We stayed at an inn at "Tappahonack on the Rappahanock." His ancestors had settled on land along the Rappahanock River in the 1600s.

We went to Washington's home at Mount Vernon. One of my father's forebears had been an aide-de-camp to Washington during the Revolution, and I like to think the old fellow would have enjoyed knowing the little girls who played so happily on his green lawns belonged to him in a way.

We visited my father's boyhood home in Falls Church, Virginia, and picked wild daisies in the meadow where he used to play.

My father always loved music, and one of our favorite trips was the journey to Judge Rowan's home in Kentucky, the inspiration for several of Stephen Foster's songs. He introduced us to opera and bought season tickets for the St. Louis Symphony every year when we were teenagers.

When I was twelve, we moved "up North" to St. Louis. President Roosevelt appointed my father U.S. District Attorney in St. Louis. He gained the reputation of an invincible prosecutor, winning all but one lawsuit in the twelve years that he held office.

Lawyers, judges, and members of juries never forgot his skill in court as he emphasized his arguments with pounding fists and dramatic gestures, winning his cases by the power of his logic, aided by his dominating appearance. He was only five feet, ten inches tall, but his erect, proud bearing made him look much taller. He had kept his military bearing all his life; his service in the U.S. Cavalry and Artillery during the First World War was one of the periods of his long career he was most proud of. After the war and his marriage to my mother, he had campaigned for Prosecuting Attorney of Scott County on horseback and won.

My father always found time to visit his children and grandchildren when they were away at boarding school or college, in spite of his busy career. In addition to his legal work, he served as State Commander of the American Legion, District Chairman of the Boy Scouts, and held office in many organizations.

My father was no plaster saint. He flirted with his secretaries and other beautiful women he met. He was still making complimentary remarks to waitresses and stewardesses when he and Mother took trips around the world on ships and jet planes in their seventies. He insisted Mother accompany him even after her stroke, so she wouldn't "give up."

My father loved most everyone he met and showed them that in so many ways. He invited his grandchildren to visit them every summer, after his term of office in St. Louis was over and the family had returned to the home in Sikeston.

He was proud of his eight children, all of whom had at least one degree, and many of them several degrees.

After Mother died, his health began to fail. My sister Rosemary came to look after him, bringing her three youngest children with her. An operation was necessary, and it was discovered that he had terminal cancer throughout his body. I went down to Missouri to help my sister take care of him for a few days during his recovery from surgery.

It was then that he told me why it had always been so hard for him to express his emotions in words, why he had to show his affection in other ways.

As we walked on the flagstone terrace next to the house he told me, "When I was a young boy in Falls Church, Virginia, we lived in a fine brick house, surrounded by several acres with orchards and meadows for our horse and cow to graze. My father had financial difficulties. He gave up his position with the Treasury Department in Washington, and he lost our home in Virginia. The family moved back west to Missouri. All except me.

"I stayed back East because there was no law school near the small town my family moved to in Missouri. I wanted to make something of myself. I wanted to make my parents proud of me, to make up to them for their loss. I stayed in Washington, living most of the time with my Aunt Kate. I attended Western High and Georgetown Law.

"Believe me," he continued, "I was mighty lonesome. It was very hard for me. I was separated from my family for seven years and I never had enough money to make the trip west to Missouri to see them. And they could not afford to come east to visit me. Every Christmas I spent some time crying in my bedroom. I especially missed all the birthdays and the old-time family picnics on the Fourth of July.

"I was captain of the winning football team at Western High, but not once could anyone from my family come to see me play. I was captain of the debate team, but no one came to hear me debate. I came in first running the mile in the regional track meet, but no one could be there to cheer me on.

"But what really hurt was high school graduation—I was valedictorian of my class and not one member of my family was able to be present. The same for my graduation from

Georgetown Law School. So you see, I know how important it is to make a young person feel appreciated. That's why I had to form a hard shell around my heart—to keep it from breaking. That's why being with my family as often as possible is so important to me. That's why I love you all do dearly." He had finally said it.

Six weeks later he flew to Detroit for our daughter Kaymarie's wedding. Shortly after that he had a slight stroke, leaving his left side numb. He suffered a recurrence of Parkinson's Disease, and the pain from his cancer and heart condition increased.

My father had promised to speak at a Boy Scout meeting and insisted on fulfilling his obligation. He gave his speech and drove himself home in his car. That night he had a second massive stroke, paralyzing his right side. His eyesight failed. He died a few weeks later. His funeral was on March twenty-third, exactly two years after Mother died. It was a beautiful sunny day with the Spring flowers and fruit trees he loved so dearly all in bloom. I wrote this poem for him before he died.

For My Father

The silence is silken with sadness,
With thoughts of undone deeds.
They slip in and out of your memory,
They come and go as they please.

I would take your daydreams and night dreams
And then when you awake,
I would blend them with silvery moonbeams
For a cloak that I would make.

A cloak to enfold and protect you
On a lonely path that you must take,

But first, before you begin,

I would give you all the precious gifts
That you've ever wished for me.
I would travel with you to all the unseen lands
That you've always wanted to see.

I would grow for you in your garden
All the flowers you've ever wanted to grow
And you would walk among them and love them
And all their names you would know.

The flowers are your children and grandchildren
And the dew on their petals your tears,
Tears you've shed for us through all seasons,
The harvest of eighty-one years.

I would paint you a picture so dazzling
With colors of such a beautiful hue
That all who gaze on it could feel
The depth of my love for you.

I would sing for you all the songs
That you've longed for but never heard sung
And explain all the ancient mysteries
You've pondered over and over so long.

But since all this is impossible,
Since this I cannot do,
My gift will have to be
This poem I've written for you.

Out to Get Him

A few years ago, our son Dennis was driving from his job in Chicago to northern Michigan to join us for a summer weekend. The trip took him twelve hours for the following reasons.

Dennis was traveling along M-31, observing the speed limit when an absent-minded elderly driver tried to cross from the lane on Den's right to the lane on Den's left without signaling. This old fellow's car plowed into Den's car, smashing his headlights and ruining his tires. The following excitement came next: Police, towtrucks, emergency repairs, buying new tires—the whole bit.

On the road again after six hours, there was another accident immediately ahead of Dennis. Another smash-up. One of the cars, a van, burst into flames. Den pulled the driver out of the car. More police, ambulances, etc. All of this took another three hours.

On the road again, only fifty miles from his goal, at the tiny hamlet of Levering, Den saw a blinding flash of light. He looked up. A meteor was heading straight for him. He pulled off the highway onto the shoulder and waited for the end, thinking, "Oh, Lord, I guess you really want me to die today!"

Den opened his eyes and saw the meteor pass over his head and land in a field a few yards away.

A Trip to the Cider Mill

"Good Heavens, Tom, good heavens! Why hasn't someone covered up those poor kids? Do something, oh, please do something! Shall I get out and help you? What can we do?" I screamed at him, not knowing what I was saying or doing as a shocking scene intruded and disrupted the sweet serenity of our perfect fall day.

Only a few minutes before, the anxieties and terrors of the past months had seemed far away and forgotten as we drove through the countryside, relaxing in the warmth of the October sunshine. On both sides of the road, great trees flaunted their new reds, oranges, and golds.

After a morning of chores, my husband and I were on our way to the old cider mill, driving at a leisurely pace. A sharp turn on the country road brought us abruptly into a real-life tragedy.

First we saw the flares. They were held by two men, passersby, as we were, who apparently, had arrived only moments before. Several teenage boys and girls were standing on the near side of a crossroads, whispering together, their faces fixed in horror and their bodies frozen. They could have been characters lifted from a modern version of the old fairy tale, "The Sleeping Beauty," so motionless were they.

But these youngsters were held in their trance, awaiting a force far more sinister than a handsome young prince to release them from their spell. For the sleep of two in the scene might last forever. Death was waiting—perhaps to claim his own.

A housewife and her husband stood silently on the far side of the road. They stood in front of their farmhouse, he, with one gnarled, weatherbeaten arm around her for support, resting the other arm and hand on the trunk of a solid oak, gathering strength from the giant tree. The oak, brushed by a passing wind, began to flail its branches in the air in seeming supplication.

Both of the farm people were immobile except for the woman's hands, which she continually clasped and unclasped as she stared at the bank of the ditch in front of her.

An old '66 blue Buick Skylark lay crushed in the deep trough of the ditch, its windshield completely shattered. Shattered by the two teenagers who had been riding in the front seat of the car. Obviously, they had not been using their seatbelts.

They had been flung out of the car and through the windshield with such force that they had fallen head over heels and landed on their backs on the bank of the ditch. By a freak of chance, they had been tossed one on top of the other. They lay with their arms entwined, as if in one last, desperate embrace. Both faces were completely covered with blood; it was impossible to distinguish their features. Were they two boys, or a boy and a girl? They both wore jeans, tennis shoes, and worn, woolen plaid shirts, like most teenagers at this time of year.

Although blood covered both faces, the hair of the one, which now appeared to be a girl, lay long, loose, a shiny brown, still clean from its recent shampoo, untouched by the red that covered the features. The slim, lovely figure was barely perceptible under the shapeless clothing. The form was so vulnerable, yet so winsome in its last agony. I thought I saw some slight movement in the body, some flicker of life trying to hang on. No sound came from either of the young people.

Tom sprang from the car, commanding me, "You stay there, honey—there's nothing you can do! And it looks like none of these people standing around here have done anything practical, either. They all seem to be in a state of shock themselves. You stay in the car—it would only upset you, and then I'd have you to look after, too!"

In a few minutes, he was back in the car.

"This is much worse than I thought, and apparently no one has called an ambulance yet. They don't seem to comprehend what has happened and what they should do about it."

We drove down the road as fast as the law would allow.

Tom parked and tore into the store, returning just minutes later. "The operator said no one had put a call in yet to the nearest hospital for an ambulance. She's summoned ambulances, police, and a rescue squad. They'll be there in a few minutes. We'll have to go back now."

We returned to the crossroads.

In just a few minutes, a car with a doctor arrived. Then we heard the welcome call of an ambulance siren. The shrill, piercing cry aroused the farmer's wife from her numbed condition. She started, then scurried to the house, returning with a soft, blue woolen blanket to cover the piteous little couple, locked in a last embrace at the side of the road.

Police, rescue cars, and more ambulances arrived.

Tom opened our car door and spoke to me again, "There's nothing more I can do here." Then he hesitated. His face paled, and the telltale nerve in his cheek began to twitch, betraying his concern. He began to tremble.

"Just a minute," he said. He went back to the twisted old dark blue Buick in the ditch. He stared at it for a minute, then returned.

"I was so busy being a good citizen, I didn't have time to get personally involved. Do you realize that could be Annie's boyfriend's car? That could be Mark's car! Did he and Annie get home from their ride in the country? Didn't they say they were going to the cider mill? What was she wearing today? Her blue jeans and old blue shirt?—That could be Mark and Annie!"

"Oh, no, Tom—don't say that! She had to be back to go on her waitress job at two o'clock." My voice tried not to betray my despair.

"Pat, honey, it was impossible to make identification. Both their faces were sliced completely off. They're dead now. I didn't want you to know. I don't remember Mark's license number, do you?"

I couldn't speak but shook my head, "No."

A wave of nausea swept over me. My right arm and hand began to go numb. I was afraid I would faint, although I had never done so before in my life. Finally I was able to get some words out, my quivering voice a stranger to me

"There's only one way we can be sure if it was Mark and Annie or some other kids. We'll have to go to the restaurant and see if she's there, waiting on table."

During the fifteen-mile ride from the fatal crossroads to the restaurant we seldom spoke. The silence was heavy with apprehension. We tried to reassure each other with an occasional forced smile. But each of us was really alone—isolated, glued to his very private thoughts.

I shut my eyes, praying silently a slightly irreverent prayer: "Please, God, we're not Job and his wife," I pleaded, "I really do think we've had all we can take this year. Please don't let it be Annie and Mark!"

My thoughts now centered entirely on Annie.

"Was this what we had nursed her through all those childhood traumas for—to end up like that—dead on the side of the road at seventeen?"

I had nursed her through all the usual childhood diseases plus a few rare and even exotic ones—scarlet fever, "Johnson's

Syndrome," an operation to remove a penny from her trachea when she was barely a year old. She had always been shy until the last year. Then she had transferred from the private girls' school where she was a student, thanks to a special scholarship. She loved the school, but had no friends to pal around with on weekends and after school during the week. Most of the girls who were friendly to her lived too far away. The girls who lived in our neighborhood and attended the school were very snobbish to her. They wouldn't even speak to her on the bus they rode out to the school, or even acknowledge her presence while they all waited at the busstop together. Her teeth had been "bucky." She had never had a date—she didn't even know any boys her age.

The change in schools had been hard at first. Her natural shyness kept her from making friends. But her sister who was only one year older was her friend and ally. She had braces on her teeth and could look forward to the day when they would be removed and her smile perfect. That day had come last week. The braces were off—just in time for a braceless smile in the high-school yearbook.

Last spring everyone in the family had encouraged Annie to try out for a part in the school play. She auditioned and got a small part. One of the boys who had a leading part in the play loved Annie. His name was Mark. He had fallen for her and didn't mind letting her know it. He took her to the Spring Prom and out for dates every weekend after.

Even though he had gone away to college this fall, he came home every weekend to see Annie. He had taken her out today—out for a ride in the country to the cider mill.

We were near the restaurant now.

"I think I'll go through the alley. Do you want to come in with me? We'll go in through the back door so we won't cause a commotion." Tom looked at me, inquiring with his eyes as well as his voice.

The car stopped in the alley. We both sat in it for another moment, each praying that Annie would be in the restaurant. Or, if not, that God would give us the strength to bear what we had to.

Slowly we got out of the car and made our way to the back entry. We peered into the darkened interior. There, in the bright glory of her crisp white uniform stood our darling Annie, bending over to unload a tray on a customer's table, her beautiful shining brown hair tucked neatly into the necessary hairnet.

Somehow, she sensed our presence and straightened up. She turned toward us, showing her sweet, straight-teeth smile,

"Mom and Dad, what's the matter? Did you want to buy a Coke or something? Why are you crying?"

Setting the Table for Brunch

Our daughter, Rosemary, who lived in Ireland for seven years, belonged to "The American Club," a group of American wives of native Irishmen. She had decided to take her turn at hostessing the group for brunch because I was in Ireland for a visit and could help her with the project. She was the mother of little Annie, a very active two-year-old, who, in spite of her age and small size, had become the "boss" of the neighborhood preschoolers.

Rosemary and I had set the party table with her best china and silver. Annie was very interested in the unusual activity. She climbed up on a chair and leaned over the table. She began to rearrange the china. Her mother commanded, "Annie, please get down before you break my good china!"

The two-year-old gave her mother a long hard look and then replied, "No, Mommy, I will *not* get down. I have a life of my own to lead, as well!"

Anna's Fifth Birthday Party

Anna's real birthday was last week, but since her best friend Emily was out of town, the birthday party is being held today.

My daughter-in-law, Sandy, two grandsons Tommy and Sean, and I arrived in East Lansing early, in time to give a little assistance to my daughter Maureen, Anna's mother. And in time to catch snatches of conversation from a telephone call.

Rachel will not be able to attend the birthday party because she and her two siblings are sick again. Rachel is crying and fighting with the two-and-a-half year old who is biting her eight-month-old brother. Oh well, three fewer children may cut down on the biting and fighting for the afternoon ahead.

Anna, her little sister Mia, Tommy, and Sean run outside to play. Anna falls down, scratches her knees, and splits her lower lip. Next she gets a big goose egg from bumping her head on the newly polished sliding glass door. Mother Maureen has just removed the peanut butter and jelly smears and messy fingerprints from it. It is so clean that Anna can't see it. After this latest tragedy, Mom, Grammia, and Aunt Moonie furnish the necessary hugs and kisses, and all is well for a few minutes.

Now the other guests arrive, including dear little Emily. We serve them ice cream, cake, M & M's, juice, and birthday favors. These are yoyos. My grandson Tommy stares at his for a moment and says, "I don't know how to use this thing but it would make a great wrecking ball. I think I'll try it on somebody's furniture after a while!"

One little girl blows out the birthday candles before Anna can work up her wind.

"That wasn't very nice, Mary Lou," Anna remarks as tears fill her eyes. We light the candles again, and this time Anna beats Mary Lou to the draw. Now Mary Lou cleans her plate ahead of all the others. "More ice cream?" my daughter asks the little girl.

"More ice cream? I hate it!" Mary Lou replies.

The children play pin-the-tail-on-the-donkey and other birthday party type games.

"May I please open my presents now, Mom?" Anna asks, pulling Emily to her side.

"Yes, Anna. Now all you children sit in a circle around Anna, and she'll open her presents."

Anna opens her gifts. All the children grab for them. Before Anna can play with them. Most popular of all is a large box of brightly colored beads. These little girls make bracelets and necklaces. Tommy makes an enormous long snake. The snake fascinates Mary Lou. She pulls it out of Tommy's hands.

"You maniac!" Tommy yells at Mary Lou and grabs the snake back. It breaks into dozens of beads. They bounce all over the floor. This episode ends in an apology from Tommy since his mother is present. Mary Lou's mother is *not* present, so she does *not* apologize, naturally.

The children sing songs, fight, and scream a little more. Every time Emily and Anna try to sit or stand near each other, Mary Lou elbows Emily out of the way.

Anna, the little hostess, bursts into tears again, and her mother carries her upstairs for a long overdue nap while the hubbub continues downstairs until the last parent collects the last child.

Now my daughter Maureen drags herself and little Mia up to bed, too, and we depart for home.

Niskey Lake Trail

"Mornin', Miss Patricia." The soft voices of several men and women greeted me through the early hours as I chased my toddlers up and down the gravel driveway and through the gardens and orchards that filled the acreage of my childhood home.

The men and women ambled down the driveway past the playground, with its old broken swing set and slide. They moved around the derelict barn, empty now except for the occasional stray cat and litter of kittens. The visitors were walking to the bamboo grove behind the barn and then back again.

My Uncle Milton had given bamboo shoots to my father when he returned from his tour of duty in Japan after World War II. The bamboo had really taken hold and flourished in the fertile soil and almost tropical climate on my father's property near the Missouri Bootheel. During my yearly trips home, I watched the bamboo grove spread until it covered about half an acre.

Bamboo made wonderful fishing poles. My father's grove supplied the local residents with their fishing gear. Anybody who wanted to go fishing and needed a pole was welcome to help himself or herself at Mister Harry's place. Many an expert fisherman honed his skills courtesy of Milton's bamboo.

I knew that Uncle Milton had been a professor at Georgia Tech in Atlanta, heading the Economics Department. But I never really knew what his role was in Japan. I thought he had served in some diplomatic capacity, but I wasn't sure.

Uncle Milton had always been my favorite Blanton Uncle, even during my childhood. He never teased me and threatened to cut off my ears with his pocket knife as Uncle Ben, the engineer, had done. He wasn't outrageously funny and witty like Uncle Charlie, the town's newspaper editor. *His* reply to the usual greeting, "How are you?" was often, "If I felt any better, I'd be dangerous!" Uncle Milton wasn't as handsome and attractive as Uncle David, a lawyer. But he *was* very good looking, charming, interesting, and very kind. I realize now why he was always my favorite among the Blanton uncles. In appearance he was almost a carbon copy of my father. Only Uncle Milton was relaxed, easy to talk to, and open to suggestion. My father was reserved, dignified, and somewhat rigid in his ideas. He expected his children to be perfect, which was, of course, impossible. He died in 1973.

When I was in college in Washington, D.C., Uncle Milton was often in town on business and would take my sister Rosemary and me out to dinner and be our surrogate father for the evening. But I really didn't know what an important person he was.

Although he often visited our family in Missouri, I had never had the opportunity to visit him and Aunt Polly at their home in Georgia. When my younger sister Anne suggested that she and I make the trip to Atlanta five years ago, of course I agreed. At that time Uncle Milton was eighty-two and Aunt Polly was eighty.

Anne flew from Memphis and I flew from Detroit, and we met in the ultra-modern ultra-intimidating Atlanta airport. Uncle Milton had warned us he wouldn't be waiting at the airport for us. It was impossible for him to find a parking place close in and too hard for him to walk a long distance. He had suffered two slight strokes during the prior year. So we called him at his home on Niskey Lake Trail. We were waiting at the airport entrance when he pulled up in his car.

I had forgotten how much Uncle Milton looked like my father. The same heavy, bushy eyebrows. The same thick luxuriant white hair. None of the Blanton men ever went bald, even in their eighties. He had the same brilliant true blue eyes as my father. They were the kind of eyes that caught *your* eyes and then locked them in. He said, "Wonderful to see you sweet things." He had always called me "sweet thing" or "honey bunch" or "precious," as had my father. Uncle Milton had arrived alone. Aunt Polly wasn't with him.

"Polly has been busy in the kitchen and was too tired to come with me. I told her to rest a bit before we got back," Uncle Milton continued.

The trip to their home was beautiful. After miles on the highway, we turned onto Niskey Lake Trail. Although it was already November, Georgia's Autumn was just beginning. The hardwoods on either side of the trails were blazing with scarlet and gold. They were especially brilliant because of the delightful southern sunshine. The day had been gray on gray, cold and gloomy when I left Detroit only a few hours to the northwest by air.

Having never seen a picture of their home, I had preconceived ideas of a southern-home type with the expected white pillars like my Grandpa Blanton's home, only much larger and grander. I knew Aunt Polly's maiden name was Swan and that her family had been one of the pioneer families in Georgia.

Finally we drew up to their property. Five acres beautifully landscaped. The house was not the stereotype white southern mansion with pillars, but a much more modern one-story ranch type, which went on and on and on and on with many rooms. There was a wonderful new addition, which they had added to their retirement home on Niskey Lake. The addition was an exact replica of the paneled library-den of their former home.

Atlanta had grown around their former twenty-acre property where exotic plants, bamboo, and thousands of varieties of iris brought back from Japan had made their home a real show place.

"I wondered what your house would be like, Uncle Milton. It's beautiful," I said as he gave us the grand tour. The house was filled with elegant furniture, much of it antiques from Aunt Polly's family.

"The other place has been turned into a subdivision," Uncle Milton said.

"I'd love to see Aunt Polly's family's old home," my sister Anne interjected.

Uncle Milton chuckled. "I'm afraid y'all are way too late to see that. It was right downtown and was sold long, long, ago to Sears, Roebuck, and Company. The property is now their parking lot. It wouldn't be much of a thrill to look at a bunch of cars! I'm sure Patricia has seen *enough* cars, right, Honey Bunch?"

This allusion to cars because I lived in the Detroit Metro Area would creep up in our conversations later on, but he was wrong about my having seen *enough* cars. I loved cars. Some of my favorites from years past flashed through my mind—the unforgettable electric car that my Grandma Daily had driven until she was eighty, the Chevy with the rumble seat that took our mother, daddy, and the three oldest girls on several vacations through the southern mountains, Tom and my first little Ford, bought with Tom's pension after his separation with the rank of Captain in the Army Air Force at the close of World War II.

Aunt Polly greeted us with hugs and kisses. She was still stunning. Her gorgeous white hair still long and thick and wavy and piled into a stylish bun on top of her aristocratic head. She had prepared a delicious casserole. Anne and I did a quick salad job with fresh vegetables. Before we sat down to dinner in the cozy kitchen, Uncle Milton had stirred up highballs for Anne and me and himself, which we carried to the library to sip while the casserole was heating in the oven. Aunt Polly couldn't have any alcohol because of her strict heart disease diet. But she got around that by taking over his ice left at the bottom of his glass. She sucked it and said she got the good out of it. It put me in mind of a friend of mine at Trinity College in D.C. She must have reeked of alcohol when she signed herself in after a date. The presiding nun sniffed the air, frowned, and asked my friend, "Have you been drinking, young lady?" The young lady replied, "*I* wasn't drinking, but I just kissed a boy who *was.*"

Polly's arms had lost their strength, so Uncle Milton had built a round table with a convenient lazy susan in the middle. Now Polly could help herself to the different dishes without undue pain and stress. Uncle Milton told us how he and Polly had met at a dance at Georgia Tech. He was a student and she an honored guest. It was love at first sight. He was nineteen and she eighteen.

Since we were not only family but close friends, the conversation became a little more raucous than a formal dinner in the dining room might have allowed. I asked Polly to tell us some of the things that she remembered about growing up in Georgia as a child. She said, "Well, Pat, one thing that really sticks in my memory is visiting an old farm that belonged to one of my great-grandfathers in south Georgia. The fields had all gone back to timber, and we had to use an out house because at that time plumbing hadn't yet been installed in the house. But we kids didn't mind because the privy was really a grand affair. It was paneled inside with some highly polished hardwood, maybe even mahogony. It must have been set up for family conferences because there were five "necessary" holes carved into the wood. Two were parent-sized and three children-scaled."

I told them how I had settled down one of my infant grandchildren who screamed and screamed with colic. "Reenie and Ed asked me to come when Anna was six weeks old and help out for a few days. Her colic seemed to be getting worse. I rocked her and gave her five baths the first day. It was Washington D.C. 100-degree weather. The poor little thing couldn't stand it. Finally after a bath and trying the old childish lullabyes, which didn't work, I tried my last resort. It had always worked with my babies, including Reenie. It's your good old Georgia Tech Fight Song, Uncle Milton. Remember?

"With courage whipped up by my highball, I broke into the song with my tonedeaf voice:

> I'm a ramblin' wreck from Georgia Tech and a helluva engineer
> A helluva, helluva, helluva engineer.
> I like my women wicked and I drink my whiskey clear.
> I'm a ramblin' wreck from Georgia Tech and a helluva engineer!

And it worked. Little Anna dropped off to sleep for hours."

The next morning I awoke to the sound of remembered footsteps—my father's. I saw his shadowed profile on the window shade. Where was I? What was happening? It was a few minutes before I realized it was Uncle Milton returning from an early morning walk. My father had been gone for many years, and I was at Niskey Lake Trail.

Uncle Milton dropped Anne and me off at Mass. Afterwards he showed us the very modern and very new Wal-Mart store on our way home. We picked up Polly and went to the Red Lobster for lunch.

Later on in the afternoon, Uncle Milton took Anne and me for long canoe rides on beautiful Niskey Lake. It reached sixty feet in depth in some spots. Before he and I began our trip, he asked, "Do you want to put on a life jacket, Honey Bunch? I don't wear one myself, but you're welcome to. It won't hurt my feelings if you do." I knew he was a good experienced canoeist, but I also remembered what Polly had told me about his strokes. I said, "Yes, I'd like a life jacket." He refused my offer to help him paddle. With his strong sure strokes, we toured the lake and pulled up near his gazebo in time for a light supper.

It was there in the comfortable kitchen around the lazy susan table that I finally heard what his role had been in Japan. We were finishing supper when he looked at me and grinned. "Why, President Truman pulled me out of Georgia Tech where I was Economics Professor and made me a member of General MacArthur's staff during the Occupation of Japan. I'm the character who set up and reformed Japan's economic system. As you know, Japan is now a formidable power to reckon with. I'm afraid your friends in Detroit might think I did too good a job. Especially the automobile people." He smiled at Anne and me, the blue eyes sparkled, and it was like having my father back again.

Tomatoes, Roses, Sunflowers, Forget-Me-Nots, and Flickering Lights

Do you believe in an afterlife? I do and I'll tell you why.

Dudley T., my husband of fifty-one years, loved to plant a couple of tomato plants every summer. He would chauffeur me to Glenda's Produce and Garden Market on Seven Mile Road or the one on Grand River. While I selected various flowers plants and rose bushes, he would confer with Glenda concerning his two tomato plants.

In the early years of our marriage each summer was pregnant with hopes of those fresh home-grown beefsteak tomatoes. During the last few years he preferred to plant the sweet smaller Italian variety with the intriguing bump at the end.

While I tended to my rose bushes, patient impatiens, petunias and geraniums, Dudley T. talked to his tomato plants, urging them onward to produce the first and most succulent tomatoes in our neighborhood in the Lola Valley area of Redford Township.

Several of our rose bushes were killed during the severe winter of 1992–93. My favorite, an old-fashioned fifty-year-old, pale-pink climbing rose with a fabulously delicious scent was definitely dead. For the next three years, not a speck of green leaf appeared on the gnarled old veteran, although I watered it hopefully and talked to it often. My husband was almost as disappointed as I was that the dear old rose bush had given up.

This past year of 1996 my husband, a tax consultant, "called it quits," too, on April 15th, the final date of income tax filing.

After the funeral, I was very busy trying to cope with his absence, handling all the necessary paper work, designing his monument and supporting and being supported by our eleven children and twenty grandchildren. I forgot to plant the tomatoes although last summer I did plant several beautiful coral-colored rose bushes in my special rose garden just outside the kitchen door.

As the spring progressed, I was thrilled to see that our three-year-dead, old-fashioned pale-pink rose bush had been resurrected. Fresh green shoots and tiny rose buds appeared on the back yard fence. I felt that my darling Dudley T. was responsible for this gift and was very much still caring for me.

To encourage the newly reborn rose bush, my daughter, Moon Seagren, and I rushed to Frank's nursery and bought a trellis for it but the trellis was so huge it wouldn't fit into her Hondo Prelude. She solved this by poking the trellis through the car's open sunroof. We made it safely back to Redford with nary a ticket from a cop. The appreciative rose bush enjoyed the trellis and grew and grew and put out many blooms. Moon also planted wildflower and sunflower seeds for me. Seventy giant sunflower plants came up and spent the summer peeking over the back fence at the neighbors behind us as they frolicked in their hot tub.

I was certain my husband was still around and active in our yard and house when a tomato plant which I had not planted miraculously appeared and flourished in my beautiful rose garden by the side door. The tomato plant produced absolutely delicious, huge, beefsteak-sized tomatoes but the shape was Italian with just a suggestion of a nipple-like protrusion at the end.

Heavenly blue morning glories covered the fence behind the sunflower garden. Zinnias, poppies, daisies, cornflowers and sweet alyssum clustered around the sunflower stalks.

In the front yard, multi-colored impatiens and blue forget-me-nots competed for space in front of the evergreens my husband and I had tended for almost forty-five years. Deep blue forget-me-nots, the color of my husband's eyes, took over beneath two maple trees we had planted years ago next to the street, beyond the sidewalk.

I know for sure that my loving Dudley T. is still around—hanging out inside our home as well as inspiring the flowers to flourish in the yard.

Dudley T. tries to censor my television viewing. For instance, the lamp by his favorite La-zy-boy chair flickers off by itself if I'm watching a slightly risque foreign film on the Bravo channel.

He and I had of late cancelled each other out politically. I remained faithful to the Democratic party candidate and he voted "independently" which had meant Republican in the last few years. Recently the lamp by his chair also went out when I was watching Bill Clinton sounding forth with the State of the Union address.

So you see, when I say my twice daily list of prayers, I end it with "May his soul and all the souls of the faithful departed rest in peace. But, dear Lord, if my darling wants to hang out at our house a little longer instead to watch over me—please let him."